HEART PINS

Emma Brattin

Thank you to: Brandon, Ryan, June, and Calvin. April, Mattie, and Alyia (my cozy cats). Tina. Journey. The staff at Polo, Jam, the Fork, and Cabos—you know who you are. My beta readers, your feedback was priceless! Kelly and bar staff. BFF Leah—your never-ceasing pep talks were irreplaceable. Diane, Mark, sisters, brother, nieces and nephews (thanks for draft reading and being patient while I disappeared into writing!). Wendy and MFA instructors (learned so much). The Japanese House and SYML for providing non-stop background music. My local printshop for all the professional looking reader copies. Random people at airport restaurants that inspired me and listened to my random babbling about Charlie. Nearly last, my SME, Jim, for verifying Charlie's career was authentic. And finally, the person that helped me figure out the name for the lawyer—that one stumped me.

HEART PINS

Emma Brattin

Heart Pins

Prologue

1968 — Old Mill, Pennsylvania

"WHY ARE YOU here, Lester?" Hank growled, stopping suddenly. Bare concrete walls echoed the incessant roar of the engines in the warehouse behind him as he turned towards the dark aisle where he noticed a familiar, lurking shadow.

Lester stepped out of the shadow he'd dissolved into hours ago and sneered down into Hank's face. A head taller than his brother, Lester had always used his size to intimidate anybody that got in his way. And right now, Hank was the only thing standing between him and his birthright. He'd planned this moment for years. He smiled slightly at his brother's nervous expression.

"I'm here to take back what should have been mine," Lester said, clenching his fists at his side. He took another ominous step forward.

Hank stumbled backwards as a look of fear flashed across his face.

"Always a pushover, Hank," Lester continued with a sneer. "Now you're trying to come clean to the town—they'll sacrifice you. You're going to bankrupt the company. Everything dad built..." He stopped talking and looked over Hank's shoulder.

"Sheesh, there you are, Hank," Hank's business partner, Peter, said as he walked up behind Hank. "Hey I need...Oh."

A surprised look spread across Peter's face as he noticed Lester.

"Peter, walk away," Hank said quietly over his slumped shoulder.

"No, Peter... join us," Lester said. Stepping to the right, Lester pulled open his knee-length coat to expose a large, chrome gun waiting calmly in his waistband. A small smile pulled his thin lips to the side.

Peter shook his head wearily at Lester's weapon and

approached Hank and Lester. He stopped next to Hank and the two exchanged a worried look then faced Lester.

The three men stared at each other for a moment, the air as crisp as a leaf in the late fall.

All in their upper twenties. Hank and Lester, brothers. Two years apart. So different. Lester: blonde, broad-shouldered, tall, angry. Hank: curly dark hair, slight, kind, caring. Peter: Hank's elementary friend, nearly as large as Lester, but calm, even, and smart. The three had been running Tucker Trucking and Freight together since Hank and Lester's dad, Tucker, died eight years ago. Lester was later banished when he got caught siphoning cash and pocketing side deals using the company name. Hank agreed to not call the cops and would send Lester a monthly stipend if Lester agreed to leave the company alone and not return.

That was five years ago.

Up until now, watching Lester show off his gun, Hank and Peter believed the arrangement had been successful.

"Walk," Lester said lifting his chin towards a row of storage containers that skirted the inside of the exterior wall.

"Lester, what do you want?" Peter asked, stepping closer to Lester. Not one to back down from a fight, Peter wasn't afraid. But he knew Lester was prone to rash decisions—and he had a gun.

"Don't come closer!" Lester pulled his gun out and pointed it at Hank's forehead. Peter raised his hands slightly to show his compliance then turned to walk down the dark row. Hank turned and followed Peter. Lester shoved the gun in Hank's back.

"Go to aisle 27. There. On the left," Lester ordered.

Aisle 27 was an awkward corner shelving area where the company stored long-haul crates high overhead. With only one way in and out, new forklift workers often got stuck in here, requiring the more experienced workers to come rescue them. The corner was not visible from any other spot in the warehouse, and the light always flickered overhead. Office workers had been caught with their lovers here. No windows meant this area was abandoned with little reliable light and no sight lines from the rest of the warehouse.

"Stand against the wall," Lester said. He gestured the gun towards the concrete corner. The crates cast dark

4

shadows that draped across the floor and partway up the wall.

"What the hell are you up to, Lester? Your son is only three! How would he feel if he knew you were here?" Hank asked, turning around.

Lester lurched at Hank with his whole weight, clipping him across the face with the butt of the gun. Hank collapsed into the floor, out cold.

"Don't ever talk about my son," Lester yelled at the fallen man. "He'd be proud of me, that's what! Unlike you and Dad." He leaned over Hank and spit on his back.

Peter decided he'd seen enough and jumped at Lester. Grabbing Lester's shoulders, he tried to use his own weight to spin Lester down to the floor.

"No!" Lester yelled, ducking out of Peter's grasp. He stumbled forward and landed hard against the crumbling concrete wall.

He spun back around to face Peter and lifted his left hand, showing a button remote tucked against his palm.

"Okay, okay, Lester," Peter said as he once again lifted his hands in the air.

"You come at me again, I either shoot you, or I blow

this whole place up!" Lester yelled, barely forming his words. He spat with every consonant and the words jumbled together. He wiped sweat off his forehead with a shaky right hand then pointed the gun at Peter. "Now sit down. No! Not there! By the shelf!"

When Peter hesitated, Lester smiled. Peter felt chills raise the dark hair on his arms.

"I'll come after James, Peter," Lester said with a sudden calm that lowered his voice an octave. "And Hank's daughter." He rolled his shoulders back and adjusted his grip on the butt of the gun.

"I. Won't. Be. Stopped!" Lester whispered, leaning his head slightly towards Peter for emphasis.

Peter knew Lester was no longer in his right mind and walked towards the shelf, eyeing Hank who was still face down on the concrete. Peter thought he saw Hank move, but figured Hank was just listening for the right time to move.

"Lester, we all want to see our kids again," Peter said shaking his head. He shrugged his shoulders and faced his hands towards the ceiling. "What do you want? How does this end?"

"I want my company back, Peter. I want what you took from me!" Lester shot back, his voice back up to an octave closer to the ceiling than the floor where he stood.

"You get a comfortable salary for no work, what else do you need?" Peter responded with what appeared like a calm voice, but he was beginning to lose his patience, and maybe a little bit of hope. He balled his fists tightly as his hands began to sweat.

"I want my kid to have someone to look up to," Lester said. He stood up straighter and pulled his shoulders back, his chin twitched to the left. "I can do better in this company. You guys are running it into the ground. I have contacts that are waiting. Shipments that can bring in good money."

"We're not doing that type of shipping anymore," Peter said, his shoulders tense. He looked at Hank again. Still no obvious movement. He knew he couldn't keep Lester talking much longer.

"No kidding! My customers are pissed. I brought in a lot of money for this company. Then you threw me to the dogs. Now those customers are coming after me," Lester spit.

Lester raised his right hand, aiming the gun squarely at Peter's head.

"Instead, you're going to pay for it. I will fix the mess you two idiots made."

1

Run in with Hen

September 1996 — Somewhere in New York State Suburbs

ABOUT TWENTY-FOUR hours, she estimated. Her shoulders were stiff. She'd been tied up about eighteen of those twenty-four hours. But again, just an estimation. Normally accurate, in control, and aware, she felt guilty momentarily. She had a goal, and yet she'd wallowed in her sickness feeling sorry for herself and throwing up every few minutes. She'd begged herself to toughen up, get a grip. But the reaction to the drugs had overcome her.

She was miserable and out of sync.

A drink at a bar. One drink. That's what it was supposed

to be. A simple conversation, a few questions...and one drink.

Charlie Winslow let out a low groan as she rolled her shoulders back, trying to ease the ache. She was still coming out of the haze, compliments of the roofie dropped in her drink. Various parts of her body were asleep and tingling. She felt weak—a feeling she was not used to.

She'd used the restroom at the bar. Made a show of asking her plus one to watch her drink. Knowing full well what would happen.

She'd *known* it would happen.

She let it happen. Asked for it. Planned for it.

"I'm getting too old for this," Charlie mumbled to herself as she twisted around, attempting to sit upright. Her mind was desperately trying to take back control, despite her body's weakness. Her feet and ankles were bound, her skin broken and sore against the abrasive rope. A few more twists and she smirked slightly as she succeeded in sitting upright, her butt on her feet.

"Still got it. Not bad for thirty-two!" Normally a smooth, mid-range voice, she was surprised to hear a broken, raspy sound come from her mouth.

Her victory was short-lived when dizziness overcame her briefly. She slouched against the wall behind her and focused on breathing.

In...and out.

In...and out.

Slowly the vertigo faded. Charlie sat up again and looked around the room, her confinement. She choked back a momentary urge to panic.

Charlie was sitting on the floor in a dusty, small, windowless room where a single, bare light bulb cascaded yellowy puffs of light that couldn't hold together long enough to reach the corners. Her blue jeans were ripped around the left knee, her once crisp white button-up shirt stained and torn beyond recognition. She sat facing a wooden door, probably hollow. She guessed she was hidden away in an older home's basement, probably not far from the bar where she'd been drugged.

Johnnie's J Bar was a local's dive bar, not meant for anything good other than a heavy-handed bartender and regular clientele. Need something illegal done? You can find a thug there. You want drugs? Someone there knows someone. Not a place Charlie goes for fun. But if she's looking for a missing person and needs answers? Johnnie's J Bar had a guy for that, too.

Karl, one of those dive bar regulars, agreed a few years ago to snitch for her occasionally in exchange for not being arrested during a money laundering sting. He'd sniveled like a mouse in a trap when Charlie had told him he was being arrested and immediately suggested a regular trade of information for his freedom. As an FBI agent, Charlie knew the value of money and despite the snot dripping out of Karl's pointed nose, she'd looked him in the eye and told him if he failed her, she'd kill him.

Charlie had heard recent rumors that Karl was back into his old riff but worked for a new boss now, some guy the streets called Hen. Hen liked to involve himself in really, really bad stuff.

A newly formed subdivision of the United States Central Intelligence Agency, National Resources Division, was recruiting a foreign dignitary to voluntarily report activities to the USA, assisting the CIA in monitoring that area of their country. The day before the foreign dignitary was supposed to return home, he reported his daughter, Adtel, kidnapped. The case was immediately transferred to the Albany, New York branch of the FBI where Charlie worked, due to limited CIA resources in the area.

Charlie's field office believed this new boss guy, Hen, kidnapped the teenager. She was given forty-eight hours to find the girl. Her team went to work and decided it was time to call Karl. If the rumors were true, he'd lead Charlie directly to Hen. He'd probably also let Hen know the FBI was sniffing around. Trying to please all masters was Karl's specialty.

Through their secret way of contact, Charlie told Karl to meet her at Johnny's J that night at 10:30 PM. She didn't receive confirmation, but she knew he'd be there.

It was said that Hen was big on bribing and made no hesitation to kill local law enforcement should they get in his way—he'd certainly be interested if the FBI was on his case.

Karl didn't disappoint Charlie. Within a few minutes Charlie told Karl what she needed and excused herself to use the seedy restroom. Karl had looked at Charlie in shock, then at her drink, then back at Charlie. Charlie walked away anyway, grimacing inside and steeling herself for the next part of this ridiculous plan to retrieve Adtel.

Karl did exactly as Charlie expected and roofied her drink.

Charlie was known for taking large risks and creating incredible plans on short notice. That was *her* specialty. And she had a success rate of 98% to show for her risks, although that two percent still haunted her.

Twenty-five hours.

Charlie groaned as her stomach rolled again, reminding her how she'd been violently sick just a few hours ago.

After the bar she'd been held in the trunk of a large car for five hours. Her stomach rejected the drugs in wave after wave. Her curly hair was dangerously close to the contents of her stomach as she tried to maneuver the limited space of the trunk. The hours had passed like molasses. Her mind yelled at her for taking this case. She told herself this was a stupid way to get involved, and the possibly dumbest idea she'd ever put into play. She sort of remembered kicking the trunk and screaming for help in the depth of her misery and stench. Fortunately, nobody had come to rescue her.

Finally, as her stomach had begun to settle and the

humidity making the space nearly unbearable, the trunk of the car had opened and fresh air flooded in. It was dark outside, so Charlie couldn't make out the features of the large person that reached into the trunk.

As her captor roughly blindfolded her, she noticed the roofline of an industrial building to one side, and a row of trees to the other. Hands encircled her narrow waist and yanked her out of the trunk as if she weighed nothing. She allowed the captor to pick her up and remove her from the mess and stench she'd left behind. She quietly sucked in fresh air but remained limp through the short walk and perhaps even passed out.

Suddenly the hands left her waist, and she awoke as she was tossed into a cool, shallow pond. Her feet found the slimy bottom, and she shoved herself up to the surface, despite her hands tied behind her back.

"Hey!" She croaked and coughed, the blindfold still intact despite her plunge. She heard a deep voice chuckle then meaty hands grabbed her shoulders and dragged her out of the water.

Did he want me clean or awake? Charlie thought to herself, still coughing up water from her lungs.

She found her footing and crossed what felt like a grassy space, through a structure, and down steep stairs. A few more steps and the hands pushed her down on a concrete floor where she blacked out again.

Twenty-six hours.

Awakened from dozing by the dull thud of heavy-footed boots approaching, Charlie sat up straight in the concrete room. Fully dry from her plunge in the water, she leaned forward, allowing her legs to stretch straight out. She reached forward for a moment then pulled her knees back up to her chest. She rolled her shoulders back again now realizing her blindfold was nowhere to be seen. Had she been moved again?

The steps stopped and the door swung inward, the movement scattering dust across the floor. A heavyset man stepped in, ducking to get through the doorway. *Definitely a henchman*, Charlie surmised to herself. His body might appear to be overweight, but she knew better. Beneath that weight was pure muscle. No matter how much physical training she'd gone through, this was not a man she'd pick a fight with unless she had a weapon.

"About time you woke up," the large man said, glaring

at her. "Boss wants to see you."

The large man stepped over and grabbed her arm, yanking her to standing. His right hand was so large, it could have wrapped around her left bicep three times.

A different hand than the one that brought me to this room, she noted.

"Oh fun, a call boy," Charlie grunted, hopping awkwardly to keep up with her left shoulder as he hauled her to the door. "Aren't you going to untie my feet?"

"Nope," he said. He headed towards the door with her in tow. "Better hop faster."

Charlie made it five feet across the concrete floor before she missed a beat in her hop and her knees crashed towards the floor. The henchman let go of her arm and grinned as he watched her fall. She tried to land against the wall to break her fall, but her hands tied behind her back gave her no balance and she landed on the concrete floor, her right shoulder and the side of her head taking the full impact of her own body weight. She swallowed a painful cry, momentarily shocked. Her shoulder throbbed.

Breathe, Charlie, she reminded herself.

In...Out.

"Up!" Her captor roared; amusement dissipated. He snatched her off the floor, this time with a beefy hand on each of her arms. He pulled her arms up and behind her, her shoulder screaming in resistance. The side of her shirt split open, exposing her torso.

"You're lucky my mother is dead, she'd have your head for ripping my shirt like this," Charlie muttered through her teeth. "This would be a lot simpler if you'd just untie my feet!" She willed her body upright, trying to relieve the pressure from her shoulder. The right side of her head throbbed from the impact of her fall.

"Where's the fun in that?" He responded. But he hesitated for a split second, glanced at the stairs in their path, then seemed to come to some sort of conclusion. He released her with his right hand, allowing her right foot to touch the ground. Shoving his hand in and out of his pocket, he flicked open a hunting knife with his thumb. She raised her chin slightly to show she wasn't afraid of him. He chuckled at her defiance then squatted down reaching for her ankles.

She twitched as he clipped the skin on her ankle bone with the blade while cutting the rope. She'd have loved to tackle him or kick him while he was hunched over, but even in that position he was still up to her chest. At 5'8", she wasn't short, but he also outweighed her. Despite this knowledge, she resisted the urge to fight as blood dripped down her ankle.

"There. Now, move," he mumbled with a grunt as he lifted his mass off the floor. He grabbed her left arm tightly and pushed her through the dimly lit hallway. The air stung the rope wounds on her ankle, and her weak body reminded her she hadn't walked in about twenty-five hours. She felt either drunk or as if she hadn't slept in four days. Nonetheless, she told her feet to go forward, one after the other.

Focus on the goal, she reminded herself. *Breathe.*

Charlie was grateful that her mind had cleared. She'd never felt off her game like she did those first few hours following the drugs.

Charlie stumbled towards the stairs, passing various doorways. She glanced left and right as she passed. Each room similar to her previous concrete prison. Charlie glanced in the last doorway at the bottom of the stairs as she lifted her right leg to meet the first stair step.

An adult male was sprawled on his back in the middle of the room. His chest had suffered a gun shot wound from a large bullet. The concrete around his torso was stained a dark red and the smell of rotting flesh hit her in the face.

Charlie's mouth dropped open; her heart doubled its beat. Her foot missed the step, and she would have fallen forward but the large hand kept her upright. Charlie felt like she might be sick again.

She leaned her head forward and choked back a scream. Her mind wandered back to the moment...

Tim was in charge of planning date night this time. He'd chosen to cook together...for the second time. He would teach Charlie how to make his family's lasagna, he'd said. Wine, dinner, some laughter—a perfect way to defuse and celebrate their recent engagement. She hadn't been able to reach him today but figured his job kept him busy, too. As she approached their front door, she stopped to fluff her long, curly hair and decided to add some lip gloss as a last-minute thought. She was dabbing her lips with her middle finger when she froze. The front door. It was slightly ajar. Tim! Charlie quietly pushed open the door with her left fingertips, drawing her gun with her right hand. As the door opened fully, Tim was lying there, in the entry way, on his back. Arms spread above his head. Dead. The chest wound gaping. Charlie screamed in pain, in terror, in anger. An emotion she'd never felt surfaced.

"Lady!" Her escort yelled, forcing her to face the staircase.

Charlie put one foot forward, begging herself to ignore the painful memory that the dead man surfaced.

"Who was that?" Charlie said shakily, trying to still her heart and her emotions.

Breathe, Charlie. In...and out.

"What are you, dumb?" The man replied. He shook his head and propelled her up the worn, wooden stairs.

She focused on the creaking of the stairs. The way the wood bowed under his weight made her hope the stairs didn't collapse under them.

One step at a time, she said to herself as she focused on regaining emotional control.

"Ah, Karl," she said frowning as she realized who the dead man in the basement was. At least it wasn't the missing girl, Adtel.

"Bingo."

Charlie sighed. She'd wanted to kill Karl herself a few times, even threatened it.

"What did he do to finally reach his demise?" Charlie asked quietly.

"Boss said he gave you too many drugs, so you made him miss a deadline. Boss doesn't like missing deadlines. I'm sure you'll get the same treatment," the man replied with a nondescript tone, as if they were merely discussing the weather forecast.

"What deadli..." Charlie started.

"Ssh," he interrupted as they reached the top of the stairs.

The pair entered a room that looked like it would have been used as a living room. Three plastic chairs in various positions were the only furniture. Two of the chairs bowed under the weight of large men who looked similar to her escort. The green shag carpet below her feet looked original to the house, probably late 1950s. Several bare spots showed a common foot path through the room. The front door was to Charlie's right, a hallway to the left probably leading to a kitchen. Most houses of this age had similar floor plans.

The man half-dragged, half-led Charlie to the remaining white plastic chair in the middle of the room and dropped her into it. She landed hard on her hands and tried not to grunt out loud. Her escort chuckled again and walked out of the room, down the hallway. Charlie heard a door shut.

The two men stared at her. She stared back but took the moment to evaluate her physical strength.

Her shoulder was certainly injured, perhaps just a bone bruise. Although the swelling told her she probably had a fracture, or worse. Her ankles and wrists ached from various lacerations and rope burns. She had a bump on her head, perhaps a light concussion. She was a little dizzy but felt clear enough.

It was time to focus on getting information about the missing teenager.

She gazed at the men before her. One was a spitting image of her escort, probably a brother or first cousin. Huge broad shoulders, linebacker body, beefy hands—

solid muscle. The other guy was big but not as large. His shoulders slumped forward, and the grey hair suggested he was a generation older. Uncle? Dad?

What a fun family event, Charlie thought sarcastically.

Charlie looked down at her lap, took a breath, then up again at the older guy.

"What do you want from me, Hen?" She asked sternly, looking directly into the older man's face.

In response, the younger man jumped up from the chair and deftly took one step across the room. He smacked Charlie across the face with such force her chair tipped to the right, and she sprawled across the floor.

"You don't speak until spoken to," the man growled. His voice was higher pitched than the other man, and much angrier. He seemed like the kind of person that barely managed to cover up years of resentment and angst.

Charlie whimpered as she tried to move to sit up, her eyes unable to focus on the movement in front of her. A booted foot connected with her stomach and Charlie gasped. She heaved up whatever was left in her stomach.

"Oh, that's disgusting! What the hell!"

Lying on her right side, hands still tied behind her back,

Charlie struggled for air. She opened her eyes to see where the man stood.

She briefly made eye contact with Hen as she coughed. His eyes were colorless, empty. His eyelids red and saggy, his eyebrows untamed. He showed no expression as the younger man stepped into Charlie's vision. She closed her eyes and braced herself for the next blow.

"Enough," Hen said in a low, sharp voice. "Find Neil and get the other girl ready. We leave in twenty minutes."

Charlie heard obedient footsteps leave the room. She allowed herself another moment to take a deep breath.

Breathe...in...and out.

What did Hen mean by get the other girl ready? The missing girl—Adtel? Charlie wondered.

Everything hurt. She was weak. Her body said she'd had enough; it was time to go.

But Charlie had never given up before. She always wins. This case will be no different. She will succeed.

Charlie sipped another breath.

Breathe...in...and out.

Opening her eyes, Charlie watched Hen stand up from his plastic throne and walk across the threadbare rug. He crouched agilely near her head; his hands rested calmly on his knees. His voice was smooth and low. Charlie felt like she was lying next to a growling tiger ready to pounce. She felt a chill creep through her when he spoke, and her mind screamed at her to get away. She forced herself to stay still.

"You are interrupting my plans. I'm not above killing a federal agent. And as you noticed, Jones likes to take out his anger on people like you. Fortunately for you, you may prove useful. If you try anything, I won't stop him next time. Got it?"

Charlie nodded solemnly. Despite the pulsing pain behind her eyes, her lungs were refilling with air. She knew her time to fight was coming.

Twenty-six hours since meeting up with Karl at the bar. Four more hours until the calvary arrives.

2

Decoys and Ragged Carpet

CHARLIE HAD SWORN to her team she only needed twenty-four hours to locate the girl. But as she lay on the ground with her wrists bound behind her, she felt grateful the team told her thirty hours...she'd certainly underestimated the volume of drugs she'd be given and the beating she'd take.

How do I keep these idiots occupied for another four hours?

Hen returned to his plastic perch and settled into a part sleep, part glare at the ceiling state of mind. Charlie wouldn't be able to do any damage to him in her current state, and she didn't know how close the other two men were or when they'd return.

As she allowed her body to rest, her head still on the itchy green carpet...her mind drifted to Tim and the first time he'd convinced her to cook with him.

May 1994

"I don't know how to do that," Charlie said with her arms crossed. She felt vulnerable, attacked, completely out of her space. "I can fix the seam on your stupid Hawaiian shirt and add another button as your shorts become too tight, but don't ask me to do that."

Tim chuckled and dried his hands on a grey dish cloth by the sink. Turning off the faucet with the towel, he glanced back at the shrimp strainer in the sink.

"Charlie," Tim said as he approached Charlie. He stopped in front of her and a gentle smile creased his eyes. "I'm not asking you to perform open heart surgery. Deveining a shrimp is much simpler, albeit annoying. Let me teach you, Love. Please?"

Charlie sighed as Tim put his hands on her shoulders and looked her in the eye with a soft smile. His hands were still slightly damp, and she felt his warmth on her bare skin.

The tank top she wore was great for hanging in around the house, especially in the poorly ventilated kitchen. Their shared condo was only five years old, but clearly the design hadn't been well thought out. When Charlie first met Tim, he'd just put down a deposit and signed the purchase on this condo and Charlie was more than willing to give up her apartment "across the tracks". But after living in the house for just a few weeks, both Charlie and Tim admitted the design was severely flawed. The kitchen didn't get much air from the central vents. If the half bathroom door was left open, the front door would slam into the door, and they'd get jammed together. The master closet doors never slid open properly. The list went on.

Nonetheless, they'd made the space their home. Charlie had never owned a home. She'd taken great care of her apartments over the years, but she'd always lived in derelict neighborhoods that likely had never seen better days. She liked to remain a nobody and those types of areas left her alone. In this condo, she found she had an eye for aesthetics and rearranged a chair here, a picture frame there, and now their place could be photographed for a magazine.

"Alright, I'll try. Sorry," Charlie admitted, telling herself to lean into Tim's outstretched arms. Tim was kind and understanding. Charlie was certain she loved him.

"You don't have to apologize. It's human nature to feel self-conscious sometimes, especially because I'm such an excellent cook...you can learn in my shadow," Tim stepped away from Charlie and blew a Chef's Kiss in the air with his fingers together.

Charlie couldn't help but laugh.

"And yet who taught you how to make stuffed chicken marsala?" Charlie shot back, poking Tim in the stomach.

Tim grabbed Charlie's wrist gently and pulled her against his chest.

This is the person I should love my whole life, Charlie said to herself.

After all, Tim was the first person she'd ever told about Mother, and the first man she'd ever trusted enough to live with.

He brushed her curls off her bare shoulder and kissed the freshly vacated area.

He is the One, Charlie reminded herself with feigned confidence.

Charlie put her head against Tim's ear and leaned into his touch. She ran her fingers across his balding head and down his neck. She squeezed his shoulder and kissed his ear.

I do love this man.

Tim stepped back and pulled Charlie after him.

"Let's do this," Tim said heading back to the black marble sink where the colander sat with freshly rinsed, orange-colored shrimp.

Tim patiently walked Charlie through the steps of deveining shrimp and how to rinse out their digestive system. Charlie cringed a few times but steeled herself against the black and brown mixture that came out like a sidewalk-baked worm. They laughed as the third shrimp slipped out of Charlie's hand and shot over the counter and slapped into the window. Tim poured Charlie and himself a glass of Willamette Valley Cabernet and they cheered that Charlie accomplished deveining four shrimp, then five, then eight. Charley felt momentarily relaxed, in the moment, a state of mind she was not used to.

"That's probably enough," Tim commented as they finished the tenth or maybe twelfth shrimp. "Let's save the rest for another meal."

"I'll get a Ziplock bag from the pantry. I lost track of how many we did," Charlie said.

"Let's blame the wine," Tim said. He smiled at Charlie with an expression she wasn't familiar with. She tilted her head at Tim then turned to open the pantry door.

Charlie froze as she spotted a small velvet box on the floor in the middle of the pantry. After a few moments, she glanced back at Tim. He had tears in his eyes. His face reflected passion. Fondness. Sincerity. Love.

And it was all directed at her.

"Tim?" Charlie managed.

"Pick it up, Charlie," Tim replied, nodding towards the pantry.

Charlie knelt, as if in a dream, and gathered the purple hexagon. She turned back towards Tim and held it up.

"Now open it," Tim said, this time with a chuckle.

Charlie stared at the box in her hand. She began to quiver. She'd been an undercover FBI agent for many years and never shook like this, even when facing death. This emotion was touching a piece of her she didn't know existed. She felt a little bit afraid, a little bit excited, and a lot unsure.

You can do this, Charlie, she reminded herself.

Can I? She wondered. Could she trust this man enough to give her life to him...*forever*?

"Charlie?" Tim asked, raising his arms, palms open, towards Charlie.

Charlie glanced up at Tim. Just below six feet. Slight. A smart man, a bookish man. No hair left to speak of, some say due to wearing ball caps his entire life, he blamed it on genetics. He was a gentle human being with the ability to look past someone's callous exterior and find their beauty inside. His lawyer experience gave him a sharp eye to see what lay beneath. Charlie loved that ability in him. *But for the rest of her life?*

Move, Charlie, she said to herself. *Don't hurt this man, he deserves this*.

She took one step forward.

Then another.

Every step felt strange, like a forced choice, unnatural, to total permanence, no going back.

Is that so bad? No, this is what adults do. We find someone we're compatible with, someone who won't hurt us, and we build a life.

Charlie reached Tim and again held the box up at chest height. She flipped open the lid to find a delicate solitary diamond with a thick gold band. It was a beautiful ring; it suited her perfectly. She'd never worn jewelry, but this one, she could get used to. Simple but classic.

"Charlie," Tim began.

Charlie was surprised to feel tears approach her eyes. She looked up at Tim and found his tears had now reached to his cheek bones.

"Charlie," Tim said again, this time choking back a flood of tears, "you are something else. You're strong, guarded, incredibly fantastic at pretending to be someone else in your job. But with me, you trust me enough to show me a glimpse of who you really are, what's inside. And I love that you love me that way. I love the work side of you, the home side of you, and now the 'I don't want to touch shrimp' side of you."

Charlie half cried, half gargled a chuckle. She tried desperately to control her tears, but they ignored her argument and rolled down her face. She sucked in a choppy breath as Tim continued.

"I want all those pieces with me the rest of my life, however long that may be," Tim placed one knee on the white tile floor.

"Charlie, will you marry me?"

Charlie stared at Tim's face, forgetting the tears rolling from her eyes.

Forever. Forever. *Forever.*

Am I capable of forever??

She began replaying all the words Tim had said to her over their time together. *Charlie, I love you. Charlie you're my person. Charlie, you don't have to apologize, you're human. It's human nature to react that way. It's okay to feel that way, Charlie. Sometimes, we all feel defensive, but we're here to support each other and learn to trust each other with our real self. Our real self is human, we're all that way, we just show it in different ways, it's okay that is how you reacted. I believe in you, Charlie. You did so amazing on that case, Charlie. Can't wait to read the details when it's released to the press. Charlie, will you call me when you arrive at your hotel? I'll worry about you all night. I trust you're making the right decisions, but I worry about you. Come home, Charlie. I love you.*

"Charlie?" Tim said meekly. He squeezed Charlie's hands. She hadn't even realized he was holding her hands. She glanced down at their entwined fingers.

My body says yes. Why is my heart so afraid?

Charlie looked up from her hands to Tim's face. His blue eyes shone with anticipation.

Enough, Charlie told herself.

"Tim, I'd be honored to marry you. I love you," Charlie said, her voice sturdy and confident despite the tears.

Tim stood up, gathering Charlie into a tight hug, and buried his head in her neck. She pushed him away slightly, put the shiny gold ring on her left ring finger. She kissed his neck working up to just under his ear lobe. Tim moaned. Charlie kissed his throat then pressed her lips to his, secretly wondering if she'd survive his love.

Tim was murdered one week later.

September 1996 – Back on the dirty green carpet

Charlie was startled from her reverie by approaching

footsteps. Her cheeks were damp, the emotion of Tim's loss on the surface. She normally buried it and focused on work, but every once in a while, she was weak and felt its pain.

Jones and Neil emerged from the hallway, half carrying, half dragging, a slight, young woman. Charlie lifted her head, trying not to look too inquisitive. *Adtel? Was it really this easy to find her?*

The girl was tied at the wrists and ankles. Her straight, dark hair tangled in the rope around her wrists. She opened her eyes briefly, visibly startled at the site of Charlie lying on the ground. She narrowed her eyes as Charlie gazed back. Charlie couldn't tell if the girl was confused, scared, angry, or just exhausted. Strong woman, Charlie surmised. *Hopefully I can rescue her.* Charlie attempted to sit up, hoping she was almost done with this case. If she could push whatever negotiations were about to begin until her partner and backup arrived, then all this would be over and the girl saved.

Jones released the girl on the floor in the middle of the room. When she tried to roll onto her side, Neil grabbed her hair and yanked her upright to sitting. The girl yelped but settled onto the floor.

Jones grabbed Charlie by her left arm and dragged her across the room, positioning her back-to-back with the dark-haired girl.

Jones was the one that took me out of the trunk, Charlie thought, recognizing the feel of his hand on her arm.

Neil walked over to Charlie, kicking the toppled white chair to the side of the room. Charlie felt the girl behind her twitch at the sound. He grabbed Charlie's hair and tilted her face back, forcing her to look him in the eye.

"Play nice," Neil said. He smirked at her, chilling her down to her soul. He let go of her hair with a shove, then sauntered over to a chair near Hen. Jones leaned against the wall by the front door. Hen sat up in his chair and folded his hands in his lap.

Charlie shook her head to remove the feeling of Neil's hands in her tangled hair and wondered why they brought out the teenager.

What kind of game are they playing?

Hen looked at Charlie.

"Karl told me you could be a friend to me, that I should trust you. He brought you to me because I told him I wanted to recruit you; to test you. What a fool. It's a small town. Think I don't know every agent—undercover or not? Other people are willing to share, too. Karl was a fool." Hen tucked his chin against his chest and took a calming breath then reached behind his back and brandished a black 9mm Glock. He aimed the shimmering muzzle at Charlie. Neil and Jones leaned forward with toxic anticipation.

"And you are also a fool. So, tell me, why are you here?" Hen smiled an evil smile, knowing full-well why Charlie was there.

Charlie felt the girl shudder behind her, but the girl remained rigid, her back straight and her chin up. Charlie felt uneasy; something was wrong. Why was Hen giving up the girl's location so easily?

She's not the missing girl I'm looking for, Charlie realized with a cold chill passing down her spine. *Who is she*?

"You already know why I'm here," Charlie said confidently. Despite the weakness and pain in her body, her voice did not betray her. Charlie tipped her head towards the girl. "Let her go, she's no use to you."

"I have a shipment I need to pass through a certain airport tonight. You will arrange its safe passage with your country and in exchange I will return the girl."

"I will see what I can do, but you have to let her go, first. You can keep me as ransom," Charlie offered.

Hen laughed from his belly, as if Charlie had told the best joke. The sound echoed off the torn wallpapered walls and bounced around in Charlie's head. Neil and Jones glanced at each other, confused.

This is getting nowhere. Let's try a different tactic.

"And you have to release your decoy, too," Charlie said, again nodding to the girl behind her.

She felt the girl suck in a deep breath.

Hen went silent and flushed red. He rotated his arm ever so slightly and released two shots from his clip before Charlie could say another word. The dark-haired girl fell back onto Charlie, then slid sideways into the floor. Charlie's ears rang from the shots. She kept her eyes on Hen, looking calm, but inside she was confused and angry. Nothing in this case made sense. What a waste to kill an innocent girl. She felt like adrenaline was going to leak right out of her body. Her heartbeat rattled through her chest.

"You didn't have to kill her," Charlie demanded, raising her voice. Her body pulsed with adrenaline. "Where is Adtel? How am I supposed to barter you a trade when the body count keeps piling up?"

Charlie felt overheated, sweat poured down her back.

"She was no use to me once you knew it wasn't Adtel," Hen smirked as if considering his next move and enjoying the drawn-out process.

Neil jumped up from his chair and looked out the window distracting Hen from Charlie.

"Uhh, boss? We got company."

3

Another Day in the Office

CHARLIE FELT JUST as surprised as Hen's facial expression showed. His mouth dropped open and his eyebrows brushed the top of his forehead.

Her team wasn't supposed to be here for another three and a half hours. *Maybe I miscalculated?* Charlie thought. *No, I'm always accurate. Although they did drug me heavily.*

"How do they know where you are!" Hen yelled at Charlie. He glared at her as though he was trying to bore a hole straight through her. Charlie stared right back, hiding her own confusion by keeping her expression neutral but she felt unnerved by the anger flooding from his eyes.

Breaking his gaze, Hen stood up and peeked out the corner of the window. He let a low growl in frustration and punched the wall.

"This wasn't our agreement! That two-timing son of bitch!" Hen stared at his fist for a moment then turned toward the silent, waiting men.

"Change of plans," Hen said in a deep, clipped voice, barely controlling his rage. "Neil. Jones. Time to go."

"What about..." Jones started.

"They're no longer useful to us," Hen interrupted sharply.

The two younger men nodded and walked down the hallway. Hen followed close behind.

"Wait, I'm sure we can make a trade," Charlie said, raising her voice as the three men disappeared from her view. She heard one of the men fidgeting in the kitchen and a brief exchange of inaudible words. "You said you need to leave the country, so let's talk!" She yelled. Her offer was met with a grunt and a cupboard door slammed.

Who are they mad at?

With adrenaline pulsing through her from her

encounter with Hen and the discharge of his gun, Charlie felt as strong as before she'd been drugged.

Nothing like some serious adrenaline to make the pain reside for a moment, Charlie thought.

Avoiding looking behind her at the fallen girl in the middle of the room, Charlie wriggled her hands under her butt and under her knees, finally bringing her hands to the front of her body. She rolled onto her left side, and tucking her feet under her body, she rolled back onto her feet and stood up. Her eyesight turned black momentarily while her brain tried to catch up with the sudden movements.

She felt every sense rise to high alert. She could hear the men's voices several rooms away, a door slammed shut. A car started. The air was warm, too warm. Sweat was dripping down her back and across her chest. Her nose picked up the smell of rotten eggs and she noticed her brain fogging ever so slightly.

Natural gas. Someone left the gas stove burners open.

They're going to blow this place up!

The hair on her arms raised.

Adtel must be here somewhere!

Assuming the men had left, Charlie threw caution to the

wind. If she didn't find this girl in less than three minutes, they were both going to die under a cloud of poisonous gas. A bad guy doesn't need bullets and machetes to take care of loose ends; all they need is a spark and a house full of natural gas.

"Adtel!" Charlie yelled, scampering towards the hallway, opposite the front door. Her cuts, bruises, fractures, and concussion were temporarily non-existent as she ignored the smell of gas and focused on her goal. "*Adtel*!"

First door in the hallway, a small bathroom: empty.

Second door, a linen closet: empty.

Third door, a bedroom: empty. No closet.

Fourth and final door, another bedroom: at first glance it appeared empty. Charlie stepped into the room and reached for the closet door.

"There you are!" Jones yelled from the hallway behind Charlie. He lunged for her, pushing her chest against the cigarette-stained wall with his body. Leaning his face against her ear, he whispered with hot breath, "I've been waiting to be alone with you." Wrapping his arm around her waist, he tried to lift her off the ground. Charlie reached her hands out and caught the rope tied around her wrists on the door handle of the closet.

"I don't think so!" Charlie cried holding onto the accidental life rope wrapped around the doorknob with all her strength.

The sudden resistance caused Jones to lose his grip on her waist, and he stumbled backwards. Charlie leaned into the wall again with her upper body and jump-kicked Jones with both her feet. Jones gawked in surprise and fell into the wall behind him.

Charlie grabbed the closet door handle again and swung it open, revealing a teenage girl with long, black hair.

"Adtel," Charlie said, breathing a sigh of relief. The girl glanced up at Charlie with large brown, frightened eyes and nodded. Adtel shrieked and Charlie ducked as Jones swung his fist at the back of her head. He missed and yelped as he connected instead with the door frame.

"You won't get out of this alive!" Jones yelled.

Charlie noticed a gun tucked loosely in Jones' waistband. As Jones swung his fist again, Charlie made a quick decision and jumped into the closet with Adtel, slamming the door behind her, narrowly missing Jones.

Charlie crouched down, shielding Adtel as Jones punched the door, nearly breaking entirely through the hollow core. Charlie reached up and held tightly to the inside door handle as he tried to turn the knob from the outside. Charlie stood up and after a few moments of tug-of-war, Charlie released her hold and shoved her body into the door with all her strength, catching Jones in the side of the head with the corner of the door.

Jones stumbled and groaned, his hands brushing the bruised cut on his head. Charlie ducked past him, retrieving the gun from his pants. She positioned her hands on the gun and started to turn around to aim. Jones spun around in annoyance, his arm backhanding her across the neck. She slammed into the wall and air rushed from her lungs. The gun skittered across the floor. Charlie paused a moment while her breath returned. Jones turned to look for Adtel and the gun, but Charlie wasn't ready to give up yet.

I won't let this innocent teenager die alone, Charlie said to herself, gasping for air.

Here comes another Charlie-level awful idea.

Charlie gritted her teeth and jumped at Jones. She

climbed up on his back and wrapped her rope-tied wrist around his neck. She struggled to breathe from the gas in the air and her injuries but refused to release him. She tightened her grip as Jones tried to shake her off. He began sputtering and slammed her against the wall again, this time his weight compressed her into the wall.

Charlie let out a small whimper. She knew she couldn't take another hit. The adrenaline fueling her fight was wearing off. The world seemed to slow around her.

Charlie saw Adtel move away from the closet just as Jones caught sight of her, too. With Charlie still on his back, he lunged at Adtel. Adtel ducked and rolled to the side, just out of his reach.

Charlie fought to stay conscious. She tried to maintain her grip, though Jones, with his focus now on Adtel, barely seemed to notice the rope around his neck. The deadly gas in the air, combined with her injuries, Charlie felt her life slipping away.

"Let go!" A young voice commanded. Through hazy vision, Charlie saw Adtel standing confidently in the corner of a room, a gun pointed at Jones. Her brown eyes were narrowed, and she was calmly aiming at her target.

Charlie didn't need to be told twice. In one last burst of energy, Charlie slid her legs up Jones' back pulling her hands up and over his head and allowed herself to fall to the floor.

Just another day in the office, she surmised as her head hit the floor. Everything went dark as a gunshot echoed through the room.

4

Stuck with Yourself

Three days later

"COME ON, CHARLIE. You've gotten yourself in some crazy situations, but that's the most ridiculous thing you've ever done," Jessica said, frowning. She straightened the stiff hospital blanket around Charlie's feet, eying her numerous bandages and monitors.

Charlie chuckled, trying not to inflict more pain on her aching torso.

"You're lucky, this time, though, you know," Jessica continued. "If Adtel had been unconscious, or too scared to help, you'd be dead. Can't believe she shot him and then dragged you out of the house. Who saved who? Maybe I'll give her your job."

Charlie smiled up at Jessica fussing over her blanket. Jessica's brown eyes were slightly squinted, and worry lines creased her forehead. Jessica became the office contact for Charlie ten years ago. She was a field agent for many years before she broke her leg on an assignment and retired from the clandestine title. Then two years ago, Greg joined the team and became Charlie's partner. Jessica skillfully organized where and when the agents went and tracked them so she could call backup if necessary. She also handled any research the field agents called in. Charlie fondly referred to Jessica as her "handler." Jessica was protective of Charlie and the two had a deep respect for each other.

"I seem to recall many stories of you doing the same thing when you were in the field, Jess," Charlie said with a smirk.

"Damn right. I taught you everything you know," Jessica relaxed her face and smiled at Charlie.

"What happened to Neil and Hen?" Charlie asked, her mind not piecing the final moments together well. She was still deep in recovery from carbon monoxide poisoning. The last three days had been a blur of medicines, sedation, beeping monitors, and a lot of sleep.

"Once we confirmed your location, Greg got antsy and demanded he and the recovery team arrive a bit early. They saw the three men exit the house and figured they could rescue you after they left, but then Jones went back inside," Jessica began.

"He forgot to say goodbye to me," Charlie said with a sly grin. Charlie mentally patted herself on the back for keeping time count despite the drugging and beatings but wondered why Greg decided to go in early.

"Greg smelled gas and insisted they go in, even though you hadn't given us the signal," Jessica continued, rolling her eyes at Charlie's remark. "When we heard a gunshot coming from inside, Greg jumped out from our hiding spot and shot Hen in the leg and Neil surrendered. Good thing, too, because next thing I know you're being dragged out of the house by a teenager." Jessica patted Charlie's hand then looked her in the eye.

"They beat you up bad, Charlie. You're going to be in the hospital for a bit."

Besides gas poisoning, multiple broken ribs, a solid concussion, and various lacerations and bruises were the prize for the successful retrieval of the teenager. Charlie felt every bit of the injuries. The old hospital bed mattress didn't help—Charlie felt like she was sleeping on a cardboard box with wrinkles. She craved her home, her gardens, her soft bed. Alone with her thoughts, she felt like she'd been thrown in prison and forgotten.

"I'm okay, Jessica. I'll be out of here in no time," Charlie responded weakly waving her hand in the air at Jessica. "Hey, remember when we went to Buffalo to meet Greg? You mentioned you needed to tell me something...what was that?" She was getting sleepy, and her brain wasn't processing reality anymore. She assumed the nurse had plunged another needle into her IV line and was forcing her to sleep, to heal.

"It was nothing, Charlie, focus on healing. I'll check in with you in a couple of days, Char," Jessica said patting Charlie's shoulder. "I'll let Greg know I saw you."

As Charlie drifted off to a drugged sleep, she wondered why Greg insisted on showing up early...

#

June 1994, FBI Field Office, Albany, New York – About Two Years Ago

"A girl's road trip?" Charlie asked incredulously. She placed a brown folder on Jessica's desk. The side of the folder had a large red stamp that read "SOLVED."

"Oh, come on, Charlie," Jessica flipped her dark hair behind her shoulder and laughed. "It will be fun! Boyd is going to drive himself, thank goodness...not sure I could be in the car with him for more than four minutes exactly."

Charlie smirked and nodded in agreement, shifting her weight to her left leg.

Gotta lighten up on those leg exercises right before work.

Nelson Boyd was the Special Agent in Charge of the Albany branch of the FBI, Charlie's base of operations. While Jessica and Charlie both respected him, he never stopped talking. His grey and white hair had accepted gravity and left his head bald and his mustache thick. A perfect frame for the lips that never stopped moving. If Charlie was filling her yellow garden-patterned coffee mug in the break room and heard Boyd approaching, she'd accept that a half cup of coffee was enough and return to her desk. Boyd's assistant would put on headphones and tell Boyd a call was coming through, even when there wasn't. Charlie admired how long the assistant could tolerate the chatter before she'd try to escape.

"Remember when I first came to this office, Boyd threw that welcome barbecue out back?" Charlie asked with a chuckle.

Jessica started laughing as she reached for the brown folder.

"Yes. Who could forget? We took turns betting on how many times he'd apologize for spitting food out because he wouldn't stop talking while he was eating," Jessica replied still laughing. "Who ended up winning that one?"

"Oh, definitely me," Charlie said confidently, "and I'd only been in this office for two weeks. I was a quick study."

Jessica put the folder with the red stamp in the filing drawer of the stained wooden desk where she sat.

"So, how about it? Can we carpool? Promise I won't apologize if I spit my food," Jessica asked, settling her laughter into a wide grin. She stood up from her desk and reached her left hand out towards Charlie, a new brown folder in her hand.

Charlie didn't move for a moment as she studied Jessica's face.

Jessica was naturally tanned with straight, black hair that reached nearly to her waist, and brown eyes that were smart but delicate. Jessica hadn't stopped her physical fitness routine despite the injury and had long toned muscles, but more voluminous curves than Charlie. Both women learned to respect the other and Jessica understood Charlie's nature to break the rules. She knew when to discipline Charlie or give a secret nod of approval. Jessica was protective of Charlie and often stepped in when Boyd got involved during a case.

With a nearly silent sigh, Charlie nodded her head. Her hesitation wasn't because she disliked Jessica, Charlie just liked her own space. Charlie was tailored, quiet, focused, literal. Jessica was energetic, vocal, happy, positive. The two women, complete opposites, were a great team. Charlie reminded herself this.

A five-hour drive with Jessica couldn't be the worst thing, Charlie mused. *I do have some wedding thoughts that I could use some input in. I'm so out of my depth planning this damn thing.*

Jessica's grin broadened, "Do we get to take the Rabbit? Supposed to be beautiful weather for June."

"Now you're crossing the line, Jessica," Charlie said playfully, trying to match Jessica's natural buoyancy. "But yes, we're definitely taking my convertible."

Jessica squealed in delight and followed Charlie to the parking lot.

#

October 1996, Kellyville, Massachusetts

Even after two weeks in the hospital, Charlie still had a lot of healing to do. That time had felt like ten years to Charlie. She became irate and impatient. By the end of the first week the nurse found Charlie passed out on the floor. Apparently, she'd been trying to do burpees. Because of the injuries, Charlie looked like she was doing a dance move where the dancer flops around on the ground like a worm. She'd passed out after two attempts. The nurse checked in on her more often after that, further annoying Charlie.

Her partner, Greg, had been sent on another case and Jessica didn't return to visit, claiming a heavy workload.

The hours in the hospital had passed slow.

Upon release, Jessica called Charlie and told her to rest at home for one week, then report to the Albany field office for her next assignment. Resting at home was easier. She had her plants, her pillows, wine, something to wear besides a hospital gown...and her car. She felt dizzy now and again, and her ribs still ached, but she was able to get back to a light workout routine of burpees, weights, sprinting, and weighted jumps. She felt herself getting closer to normal.

Charlie had no friends outside of work and no living family that she was aware of. Most days she enjoyed the solitude since she was rarely home for more than two days at a time because of work. By day five of home recovery, she was feeling restless and perhaps a bit lonely. She'd called Jessica and begged to come in early, only to be deftly turned down and told to rest.

Wandering out to the garden for the seventh time that day, Charlie hoped she'd find a weed or a dead rose head that needed pruning. She needed to do *something*. She'd watched too many movies, finished two books, and reread every gardening magazine. She considered ordering a new Glock but decided she'd ask Jessica's opinion before she mailed in the order.

Charlie kneeled in the middle of a thick section of wildflowers and reached for a red Astrid thinking she'd put it in a jar on the table. A sudden movement in the brush caused Charlie to jerk back, sending searing pain through her ribcage. A rabbit skittered to the other side of the garden, as surprised as Charlie.

"Sorry, bunny!" Charlie said to the creature and wrapped her arms around her ribs. Waiting for the pain to subside, she watched the fluffy, white rabbit stop ten feet away in the green grass to nibble something between his paws.

Great, now I'm talking to animals like a fairy tale princess. But he seems so free. Maybe I need to get a cat. You can talk to yourself and then just say you're talking to the cat. And since when am I so jumpy? Certainly not PTSD. I've been in worse situations. Maybe I'm just so ready for my next assignment!

Charlie sighed and plucked the short Astrid from its root with her right hand. Walking back to the house, she counted on her other hand how many hours left trapped with her own mind. She spotted a Queen Anne's Lace and recalled her own wedding planning and felt a pang of guilt at how she'd complained...

#

June 1994, Somewhere on I-90 outside Albany – A Couple Years Ago

Charlie smiled again at Jessica's enthusiasm of riding in the VW Rabbit convertible. After a few minutes of excited chatter and arms in the air, Jessica settled into the passenger seat. Sensing Charlie's silent thoughts, Jessica dove into the topic.

"How is wedding planning going?" Jessica asked, eying Charlie.

"I have no idea what I'm doing," Charlie responded with a sigh. "It's overwhelming. And so girly. Like why do I have to wear lace? It's tacky. Outdated. Nobody wears it anymore."

"Except for most brides," Jessica replied. "Most people are excited about their wedding...is everything okay with Tim?"

"Oh, he's perfect, and sweet, and supportive. He even

offered to hire a planner if the process was stressing me out too much," Charlie sighed again.

"That's sweet of him. I enjoy coming over to your house for dinner. You two get along well. What's the sighing about, Charlie?" Jessica asked, just audible over the breeze rushing past the windshield.

Charlie glanced over at Jessica. Her sweet brown eyes were concerned, and Charlie wondered how her sisterly relationship with Jessica meant more to her than the man she was marrying. She debated for a moment then decided to let a little truth surface.

"What if I can't love him as much as he deserves? I do love him, and I feel safe with him, I think. But there's just so much of me that I feel is locked away and I can't give that part of me to him." Charlie glanced back to the road and blushed. "That probably doesn't make any sense. I'm just a whiny person who doesn't know what she has."

Jessica patted Charlie's shoulder with a knowing smile. Charlie felt herself lean away from Jessica's hand then stopped. She smiled apologetically at Jessica.

"It's okay to recognize that part of you is struggling, Charlie. We're just humans and we have jobs that require us to shut off our emotions and sometime hurt people. Maybe that's all it is. Or...maybe he's not your person. He can be a great guy and just not be the right one." Jessica put both her hands back up in the air and sniffed the fresh air deeply.

Charlie again quietly appreciated her relationship with Jessica. Jessica said her opinion then moved on, she didn't sit and lecture Charlie. Charlie could let her in on little pieces of herself, without Jessica calling her crazy and suggesting she seek therapy. She felt calm around Jessica.

"Tim always reminds me not to apologize. Apparently, I apologize for a lot of simple things that he calls 'human nature'." Charlie spit out then instantly felt silly. She looked out the left window then back at the road.

Jessica put her hands back on her lap and stared out the windshield.

I shouldn't have said that, Charlie thought, embarrassed. *That was too much.*

"It's okay to feel that way, Charlie," Jessica began. "Although you haven't shared much about your childhood, I get that it was probably awful. You apologize for who you think you are, or how an unhealthy person might react to something you do. Sounds like Tim understands, that, too."

Charlie relaxed and smiled over at Jessica in thanks, then focused back on the steering wheel. Jessica found a radio station and both women drifted into a comfortable silence as the miles passed.

5

Relegated to Light Duty

October 1996 - Highway outside Kellyville, Massachusetts – Present Day

THE TRANSMISSION WHINED in distain as Charlie downshifted to second and leaned into the accelerator. At fifteen years old, the 1981 Rabbit didn't particularly like being driven hard, but Charlie was angry and needed the speed. The car lurched forward obediently. Second gear held a better success rate of relief than a punching bag for Charlie. The convertible top down, she breathed in the crisp Berkshire air rushing by. Her long, curly hair was clipped away from her face, rebellious ringlets bounced free in the breeze. She finally shifted into third, then fourth, wincing as she pressed the clutch. The gentle winding roads of the Massachusetts hills now her muse, she allowed the VW to rest and coast a comfortable 50 mph.

Charlie wiped away an angry tear and patted the dashboard as she slowed for the stop sign at West and Main. A drive around the hills of Stockbridge always worked to calm her down when her temper flared. Turning left towards her home in Kellyville, she reflected on how lonely she'd felt during her three weeks of recovery.

Charlie had tried a romantic relationship here and there, and even felt comfortable enough to say yes to marrying Tim. After he'd died, she'd given up trying and relied even more on work. She grieved his murder, and days like this, might even admit she missed him. Jessica was right about her taking more risks these days, but it suited Charlie. She was callous but kind, distant, but focused.

Charlie sighed, shifting into fifth. She had driven the forty-two miles to Albany this morning to receive her next assignment. As Charlie braked to turn left onto Highway 183, she reflected on the meeting earlier in the day.

"Charlie, I promise it's only temporary." Jessica said with confidence.

"That's how it always starts! Then the newer and younger come in and do a better job and the old and temporarily broken ones are forgotten!" Charlie knew she was being overly dramatic. The hospital stay, the home rest...she had a lot of pent-up energy. She was angry at this change...and maybe a little scared. "I've been undercover for years. What am I supposed to do? Work is all I have."

"It's a surveillance, no-contact assignment, not purgatory, Charlie. You go in, gather intelligence, then bring it back and write up your opinion whether they're guilty or not. It's still a case. Just no danger, no drama. No more injuries."

"I'm not broken; I can handle regular duty! I may just..."

"No, Charlie, you're *not* broken," Jessica, always so level-headed, said authoritatively. "But you're hurt. If he'd smashed you against that wall one more time, you'd be more than hurt, you'd be dead. Give yourself time to heal."

"I was in the hospital for two weeks! House arrest for another week. It was torture. And nobody was there to tell me anything about current cases or how we closed the last one. I was in the dark! If that's any premonition of what *surveillance assignment* means, I want nothing to do with it!"

Jessica flushed and Charlie took a breath. She knew it'd been hard for Jessica to see Charlie in the hospital bed. Jessica had no siblings, and she seemed permanently in awe of the hits Charlie could manage and the cases she solved. Charlie was so careful, so tailored, but secretly cared deeply about the people around her.

"It's okay," Jessica said, taking a deep breath. "You know I have your back. I won't let you be forgotten. Hell, even gimpy me is still here!"

"Jessica, I'm sorry, I know you're looking out for me, but light duty? Surveillance? Have a new agent do that! What aren't you telling me?" Charlie asked, trying to control her anger. She knew Jessica understood her frustration, having herself been removed from active duty over an injury, but she still felt Jessica was hiding something.

Jessica's brown eyes looked guilty for a split second, then she smiled gently.

"Go home, rest, read these files, and get started

Monday," Jessica said. She handed Charlie two thick brown folders and stood up, signaling the end of the meeting.

Even an hour later, pulling into her home driveway a state away, Charlie still wanted to be angry at Jessica. But Jessica's calm brown eyes gazing at Charlie in concern as she'd walked away sullen had reminded her how protective Jessica was. Jessica trusted Charlie and rarely stepped in to change her mind on anything, often defending Charlie when Special Agent In Charge (SAC), Nelson Boyd, tried to cut in and discipline Charlie for another rogue decision.

If Jessica was being this stubborn, this certain about this case...it must mean something.

Maybe Boyd is trying to get rid of me and Jessica is trying to convince him not to? No, it's got to be something else.

Shaking her head, Charlie parked the white Rabbit in the gravel driveway and looked up at her two-story clapboard house with pride. Last spring, the wrap around porch had been rebuilt and painted white, breathing life into the house. She looked off to the right side of the driveway and fondly gazed at her flower garden. Early fall, and anything that could flower was still in full bloom. Hyacinths of purples and blues were so heavy they tipped into the red twig dogwoods that stood taller than Charlie. Rose of Sharon bushes scattered the border of the gardens and showed off blue flowers of three shades.

Walking through the front door, Charlie set the brown folders on the kitchen island and poured a glass of her favorite red wine—a Bordeaux blend from a Washington State winery. Her tastebuds danced at the anticipation of the first sip. Bringing her wine glass along, she hung up her tailored mustard-colored pant suit in the bedroom closet and put on a matching floral pajama t-shirt and pants set, careful not to irritate her rib injury. Taking a long sip of the dry wine, she sighed and walked back into the kitchen. She glared at the folders then glanced over to the black and brown answering machine tucked in the corner of the kitchen next to the landline. The sight of the answering machine caused a sharp pain in her gut, and she looked away, feeling that moment as if it were happening again.

Kellyville, Massachusetts - Exactly One Year Ago

Walking up the dilapidated porch stairs, Charlie cursed herself for not leaving her porch light on before she'd left two weeks ago. She threw open the storm door and the metal smashed against the white siding. Charlie glared at the door even though she couldn't see it.

"Mother of God!" Charlie said as she fumbled for her keys and dropped her purse. Kneeling on the wooden porch in pitch black, she prayed she didn't lose her keys between the slats. She'd been planning to refinish the wood for a year but hadn't taken the time to get the process started.

"Dammit!" Charlie yelled as she felt a splinter lodge into her palm then froze as the sound of a metal rattled together directly below her feet. She knew her keys were now in the spider-filled abyss under her porch. Although she wanted to scream as loud as possible, she took a deep breath to calm herself.

Charlie didn't deal well with failure. She'd been undercover for two weeks and nearly had the intel she needed to make an arrest when her star witness was found

Emma Brattin

in pieces along the side of the road outside the local police precinct. Relations with the local force was already strained and with the FBI failing to protect the witness, the conversations that followed were brutal. Agent Boyd made Charlie take the lead in discussing repercussions with the local force and, to put it mildly, it did not go well. The local force filed a formal complaint with her field office and Charlie took a demerit on her record. Boyd stepped in and prevented a civil case from forming...and then let Charlie have it for putting him in that situation. Agent Jessica Chance came in at the end of the meeting and talked Agent Boyd down, reminding him that the FBI had nothing to do with what happened. Jessica was respectful but wasn't afraid to stand up for herself or her agents. Sometimes she stretched the truth to protect Charlie, but this time she was right. After staring Agent Chance down with daggers for a solid three minutes in silence, Agent Boyd took a deep breath and softened. His eyes turned from grey back to blue. His lips from a straight line to a simplified frown. He walked over to Charlie and put his hand on her shoulder. He squeezed gently.

"Sorry, kid," Agent Boyd said with a deep sigh. "You are

71

both completely right. I'm getting too old for this crap. Please go home and have a few days to recuperate before reporting back. That was a tough one. I'm proud of you, Agent Winslow, for how you handled yourself." Boyd rarely apologized but Jessica and Charlie knew he respected them in his own way. They also knew the reality of their jobs. Boyd had people he had to report to, too. He'd likely been tossed in a paper shredder himself.

Charlie dropped her duffle bag and briefcase on the wilted porch and slammed the off-white storm door shut. Stomping down the front stairs in the darkness, she replayed the last words Boyd had said to her.

I'm proud of you, Charlie.

She'd melted into tears immediately after Boyd spoke. Right in the middle of his office.

Jessica and Boyd stared at her like they'd seen a ghost. They'd never seen Charlie cry. Charlie never released emotion. She was tailored; her clothes always perfectly fitted. Put together, even with crazy curly hair, she always managed to look perfect. Charlie rarely grimaced even when taking a hit from an assailant twice her size. She fought passionately for success in her career.

And here she was sobbing and apologizing, looking as confused as the others.

She'd claimed she was still grieving Tim, who'd been gone for months now, and Jessica and Boyd were sympathetic.

But Charlie knew it was because nobody had ever told her they were proud of her. Let alone apologizing for being angry! She never needed that validation from another, she'd found it in herself. But for some reason, his words had hit her hard. And she'd cried in front of him.

Charlie shook her head to release the annoying replay circling her memory and marched to a small window above a basement window well. Not only had she failed at her mission, but she'd cried. Cried! And in front of Boyd.

She stepped on the wooden surround of the window well below and reached up across the semi-horizontal white siding. Wedging her pointer finger into the rotten wooden frame, she managed to open the window above her kitchen sink.

Another thing I've put off fixing.

After Tim's murder, she'd sold their flat that he'd willed to her and bought a fixer upper in the country. Her partner,

Greg had offered to help her with some projects, but she'd politely refused. She'd lied to herself about how much free time she'd have.

Charlie sucked in a breath and jumped up, her hands catching the edge of the open window and pulled herself up to eye level, her arm muscles yelling at her that she hadn't stretched yet. Inside she could see her stove, her dining table, and the corded telephone on the wall. Hoisting herself through the window sounded easier than it was, but she successfully slithered through the window and landed hands first on the yellow and blue floor mat in front of the kitchen sink. Brushing her hands off she walked across the original skinny wooden floor slats; the floor creaking its welcome home. Picking up the phone off the wall, she dialed a four-digit number.

"Hey Don. I'm sorry it's late. No, I'm okay. Please can you get me a bid to replace the front porch, the trim around my lower-level windows, and paint the whole house including the outbuildings? Yes, I promise I am okay. Oh, and I'd like some sort of motion light near my porch that automatically illuminates when I pull into the driveway or walk out the front door. Yes, Don. No, I don't need that tonight. Okay, tomorrow is fine. Thank you," Charlie said as she hung up the phone and pushed air out through her teeth.

She peered through the dark kitchen, allowing her eyes to adjust. The message light on her answering machine blinked twice, letting her know she had two voice messages from unknown callers.

Someday maybe I'll have a way to screen calls without being forced to accept their voice sounding in my house, Charlie thought irritably.

Opening the front door from the inside, she gathered her things off the porch and decided to wait until morning to dig out her keys...she hated going under the porch. She could fight off a masked man with a gun any day but facing an ant highway and spider city could wait until daylight.

Charlie tossed her duffle inside her bedroom door and returned to the kitchen. She planned on reading through her case files again to see how she missed the signs of an at-risk witness, but first she poured a glass of wine through the aerator. She learned from her late fiancé, that red wines were best when the grapes were bottled in

Washington State. Charlie also knew that his family had once ran a winery in Woodinville, Washington and he might be slightly biased. Nonetheless, she'd grown to love a good Washington-bottled Cabernet Franc or Cabernet Sauvignon.

Charlie sucked down half of her glass before she remembered the flashing lights on her answering machine. She reached out and pressed play as she took another long sip of wine. A woman's voice flowed through the living room and chilled Charlie deep to her core. She instantly wanted to press stop but she stood frozen to the floor. She considered the reality that she might shatter her wine glass in her clenched fist.

"Charlie? Charlie? Oh, maybe this is one of those machines that record my voice. Charlie? Oh, sorry. So, I just talk? Are you sure? Alright. Charlie. This is your mother. We haven't talked in a long time. I was mad at you for a long time, but now? Now I know that was my fault. I can't say sorry yet, I don't think. I think I was doing the best I could. But, that doesn't matter, I suppose. So, I hear you've gotten mixed up in the FBI...I meant that in a good way, sorry. I didn't mean you were bad. No, you're stronger than I was…. Stronger than I could ever be. Your dad… your dad. Please find answers, Charlie June Winslow. Find them. I think I explained it well? I wish we'd gone back, but you know, you left before we could. I went back. I faced it. I settled in. Your dad, he'd be proud of you. I wish he could see your new life that I picture that you created. I bet you have a cat. Maybe a boyfriend? Probably a lot of plants. I always pictured you with a garden. I hope you're happy… again, I mean that in a good way. I'm sorry, my mind is sort of a mess. The doctor said to make a call…any call. It might be my last," the voice said. It gasped, sobbed. "Charlie, I think you have a cousin close to you, please look out for him. I don't know. Charlie. Charlie. My Charlie. What have I done. Who was I? I wasted so much time. Charlie. I'm proud of you. I'm sorry. I love you."

Charlie dropped her wine glass in the sink, shattering it. The answering machine beeped to notify the listener that it had ended the first message and claimed it was beginning the next message. Charlie wanted it to stop.

"Hi, I'm looking for Charlie June Winslow," said a gentle male voice. "I'm Ralph Colmstock. I represent your mother, Patricia June Winslow. I'm sorry to inform you that Patricia passed away."

Charlie sat down on the floor, her hands shaking.

Make it stop! Make it stop!

"She has organized her affairs and claimed you as her sole beneficiary. Please call me back at the following number to set up a time to read her will. I would appreciate your compliance as I am also the executor for Ms. Winslow's estate. I have a legal right first to her and second to you. Thank you. My number is..."

Charlie echoed her mother's final words...*Your dad would have been proud of you...I'm sorry, Charlie.*

Charlie curled into a ball on the floor and let out a wholehearted confused mess of tears.

October 1996 – Present Day

Charlie shook her head to clear the intrusive memory. She felt relieved to see the answering machine was not blinking tonight. Those few months were an emotional rollercoaster of gaining a new partner, losing Tim, the failed case, and her mother's last-ditch effort to manipulate her emotions.

What if this is the beginning of the end of my career? Her mind drifted back to the brown folders as she sank into an oversized armchair in the living room and pulled a navy-blue afghan over her legs. She took another sip of wine as a slight rumble of panic set deep in the pit of her stomach. A feeling that wouldn't leave for weeks.

Maybe I do have a little PTSD from my injuries. I know I went too far on that last assignment, but that's not the first time. Just happened to be the worst time. And anyways, I got the teenaged girl back! Greg and I didn't have enough time to fully plan, we kind of just had to go for it. Weird thing was, now that I think about it, Greg didn't argue when I suggested my idea to use Karl or tell me there's another way. He was okay with me being the bait for Hen.

Well, Charlie's mind argued, *it was the* only *plan we had. And we all knew that. When Jessica heard the plan, she told me I was crazy, but that wasn't anything new. Jessica knows to trust my instincts.*

What would happen if I told Jessica I won't take this surveillance case? That she either puts me on a regular case or I'm going to another agency?

Charlie shook her head answering her own question.

No, they'd find out about my injury and never hire me. And I'm getting a little old to switch agencies anyways.

"*It's not purgatory, Charlie,*" she echoed Jessica's words in her head. "*It's temporary.*"

But something doesn't feel right.

6

A Gut Feeling

CHARLIE STARTLED WHEN her telephone rang a shrill tone from the kitchen. Setting her wine on the coffee table, she stood up too fast and grimaced as pain coursed through her rib cage.

Damn, damn, damn you, Jessica. You're right, I'm not okay. I can't even stand up from a chair, let alone run from a bad guy.

Charlie crossed the room and reached for the phone on the wall on the fourth ring.

"Hello?"

"Charlie, you're home. Glad to hear that."

Charlie recognized Greg's voice. Although always

formal and professional in his words, her partner's voice came across the line as a flirty frat boy looking to score. He looked the part, too. Tall. Broad, toned shoulders. Emerald eyes that looked through a soul instead of observing it. Strong arms. Perfect dirty blond hair kept longer and wavy on top and clean around the neck and ears. Every girl that met Greg wanted to know him. Like, *know* him. His demeanor initially irritated Charlie, but she'd learned to look past it. She was not susceptible to his charm, but she saw first-hand many times the effect he had on women.

"Yes, I was released Monday and then had a meeting with Jessica today. Are you back in town?" Charlie shifted on her feet, feeling every bit of her injuries. She wished she'd brought her wine with her to the phone. The cord was so tangled, it wouldn't reach to the chair.

"Uh, yes. I got back this morning. Jessica sent me on some CIRG that ended up being just a nut job on crack." Greg hesitated. "Look, I heard about your meeting with Jessica and Boyd, and I just wanted you to know—I'm here for you. Partners for life, thick and thin and all that stuff. So..." Greg sucked in a breath "...I'm going on this silly little surveillance thing with you. It will be a nice breather. We can get to know each other better in a slower environment, with nobody shooting at us...hopefully."

"That's great of you, Greg." Charlie managed to say. In that moment, she should have felt grateful, relieved that she didn't have to do this stupid assignment alone. Instead, she felt herself shiver. Despite working directly with Greg for the past two years, she'd never connected with him. "I'm going to leave my car at that oil change place across the street from the office on Monday then I'll be by to get a CrownVic. I should be to the office about seven-forty-five."

Greg acknowledged and they said goodnight.

Charlie let out a long sigh as she hung up the phone with Greg. She remembered the first time she met him in person just over two years ago...

#

June 1994 – About Two Years Ago

The drive from Albany rushed by while Charlie and Jessica enjoyed the fresh air and scenery. They'd stopped at a gas station in town and changed from their athletic clothes into pencil skirts, heels, and blazers. Arriving at the Buffalo's FBI field office, they parked the white convertible near a sea of black sedans. Charlie put the top up and locked the car.

"A bunch of suits, as usual," Jessica observed as she and Charlie walked into the main atrium. The tan walls, white tile, and wooden trim made the atrium look like a man's polo club. A few men in black or blue suits milled about, all looking important and uninterested in the two women standing alone in the entryway. Four oversized leather chairs flanked a chestnut paneled desk where a receptionist might sit. Several male voices drifted from somewhere down the hallway.

"This place is so stuffy and closed in. Why are we even here? It's not like we're ever going to partner with the Buffalo guys," Charlie said looking around, thinking the dusty corners could use a peace lily or some greenery.

"You know what I know, Charlie. Boyd said we are supporting the Buffalo branch as they award one of their agents the Shield of Bravery. This guy lost nearly his whole team when a case went sideways, but managed to still bring down the perp. Apparently, he's a bit of a maverick and daredevil--although not nearly as bad as you are," Jessica smiled and pushed Charlie gently on the arm. "Honestly, I'm not sure outside of that, though. Boyd is always up to something. I've been busy and not pushed him for the answer. But, hey, we got a mini road-trip out of it!"

Charlie smiled back at Jessica then noticed Albany's AIC (Agent in Charge), Nelson Boyd, walk in through the double glass doors and tapped Jessica's arm to get her attention. They both smoothed their blazers and stood up straight.

Always official, Boyd wore a dark three-piece suit and a skinny grey tie. He approached the two women so fast, his polished oxfords barely kept up. He leaned in toward Charlie. Charlie leaned forward.

"Agent Winslow, you're supposed to take an FBI issued vehicle for official business, not that ratty teenager toy on wheels," Boyd said staring Charlie down.

"Sorry, sir..." Charlie began, amusement dangling on the corner of her lips.

"No, this is my fault, Agent Boyd," Jessica interjected stepping closer to Boyd. "The only vehicle not assigned was due for tire rotation and wouldn't have been available in the short notice we had for this assignment. Next time we drive up here, I'll verify Charlie is properly assigned, sir."

Boyd nodded and leaned back, seemingly satisfied with Jessica's response. Charlie nodded back at Boyd then crossed her arms and caught Jessica's eye. Jessica looked relieved and Charlie nearly chuckled out loud. Boyd's sharp tongue didn't bother Charlie, she'd grown accustomed to his tones and enjoyed watching him and Jessica interact. After working together for twenty years, Boyd respected Jessica and rarely questioned her anymore.

"The Agent we are here to observe, Agent Greg Hamlin, is a candidate to replace Agent Topaz. With Topaz's unexpected retirement, Agent Winslow is without a partner, and we need to fill that position ASAP," Boyd continued. "Agent Chance, please follow me. Agent Winslow, please find three seats near the front of the auditorium and Agent Chance and I will join you briefly." He nodded at Charlie then turned on his heel and marched toward a closed wooden door.

Jessica seemed shocked and didn't move immediately.

She looked over at Charlie. Charlie stared back with a question on her face then shooed Jessica.

"Jessica, go!" Charlie whispered.

"But Charlie, I have to tell you something!" Jessica whispered back.

"Agent Chance!" Boyd barked, his nasally voice echoing off the ceramic tiles. He turned back around and disappeared through the doorway.

"We have the whole way home, Jess." Charlie reached out and squeezed Jessica's arm.

Jessica nodded her head and took off after Boyd, trying to maintain a professional gait and run in heels at the same time.

Charlie stood for a moment and wondered what had shaken Jessica. Charlie didn't know they were coming here to meet her new partner, and clearly Jessica didn't either. But Jessica should be used to being surprised by Boyd. Boyd didn't exactly share information until a decision had already been made.

The sudden early retirement of her previous partner had been a gut punch, and she still felt like something was off. Topaz had assured her he just wasn't up to field work anymore and wanted a new life. Then he moved away, cutting all ties to the FBI, and Charlie.

Charlie knew that even though Boyd said Agent Hamlin was a *candidate*, he'd most likely already been chosen as Agent Topaz's replacement.

"Agent Greg Hamlin," Charlie said out loud, trying on the name.

"Yes?" A husky male voice responded behind her.

Charlie instantly pictured a male model, like one that would be on the cover of a romance novel. Turning around, she knew the image she conjured up wasn't far off from reality. The man standing before her was a couple inches over six feet. Soft, wavy hair perfectly draped across his forehead, but clean around the ears and neckline. His skin lightly tanned, his shoulders broad with the shirt barely controlling the muscle. His entire body was slender but strong. Navy slacks and a short sleeve button up showed off all the right places of his body.

"Ah, sorry, Agent Hamlin. I was just informed that you might be joining us in Albany, I'm Agent Winslow," Charlie said reaching out her right hand. She noticed his eyes were a similar emerald green as her own.

"Nice to meet you, Agent Winslow. Please, call me Greg. This agent stuff makes me feel like I've vowed my life away and they erased my name," Greg replied with a perfect smile. He reached out and connected with Charlie's hand.

Charlie felt a shiver run down her spine. She didn't have time to understand why she suddenly felt uncomfortable, because Boyd and Jessica reentered the atrium through a door just behind Greg.

"Agent Winslow, I requested you to the auditorium. What is with you two agents today?" Boyd asked exasperated. The soles of his oxfords tapped as he walked closer to Charlie to reprimand her further when he suddenly noticed Greg and stopped short.

"Agent Hamlin, please excuse me. So good to see you again." Boyd reached out to shake Greg's hand.

"Agent Boyd, how kind of you three to make the trip out here," Greg shook Boyd's hand and dipped his head.

Jessica walked up behind Greg with her mouth slightly open as if she didn't believe the man in front of her was real.

"Agent Hamlin, this is Agent Chance, she'll be your field office contact in Albany, or as she's coined, your handler,"

Boyd nearly cringed as he said "handler" and gestured behind Greg to Jessica. Boyd liked things to look like his idea, and he knew Jessica well enough to know that she'd introduce herself as the handler if he didn't.

Greg turned around and Jessica looked up at his face.

Greg reached his right hand out once again, but this time his palm was face up.

Jessica smirked and set her hand on top of his. Charlie could tell Jessica was trying to be professional but was completely enamored by Greg.

Greg dipped down and lightly kissed her hand then flipped her hand sideways into a professional handshake.

"Pleasure, Agent Chance," Greg said, nearly a whisper.

Whatever was bothering Jessica earlier appeared to have disappeared and she smiled with both rows of teeth exposed.

Boyd coughed and Charlie once again held back a laugh. Jessica always had a loud personality, but she rarely bordered on unprofessional. Charlie stepped closer to Jessica and elbowed her. Jessica nodded slightly at Charlie to acknowledge her.

Despite being amused at Jessica's swooning, something

inside Charlie wanted to warn Jessica about Greg.

About a man I've never met, Charlie reminded herself.

"I must return to the auditorium to prepare for the ceremony. Feel free to yawn, I will not be offended. Agent Boyd," Greg said, tipping his head toward Boyd. He turned on his heel and sauntered to the other side of the atrium.

"Agent Winslow, Agent Chance, *now* can we go to the auditorium?" Boyd asked like he was a tired father wrangling twin toddlers. Only their long-time relationship with Boyd saved them from a lecture on professionalism in the workplace.

"Yes, sir," Charlie said and turned toward Greg's disappearing shadow. She watched as Greg turned a corner and felt relieved. She wondered why she found such a handsome man so unappealing. Not only was she not attracted to him but perhaps felt even slightly repelled by his attention.

A problem for tomorrow, Charlie told herself. She knew what fights to pick with Boyd and him choosing Greg for her partner was not one she could win.

Boyd's pace quickly overtook the women, and Jessica fell in line next to Charlie.

Jessica glanced over at Charlie and mouthed, "Oh my God!"

Charlie shook her head and shrugged her shoulders.

"Take it down a notch, Jess," Charlie whispered.

"Wait," Jessica whispered, "You just scored the hottest partner in Albany history, and you look like you ate a bad egg."

"In case you forgot," Charlie whispered back, "I'm getting married next year."

"Oh good, can I have him then?"

"No! Stay away from him."

"He your backup in case things go bad with Tim?" Jessica frowned at Charlie and batted her eyelashes.

"Jessica!" Charlie shook her head and rubbed her forehead.

"I'm kidding," Jessica said laughing quietly.

"Why did you freeze earlier?" Charlie suddenly remembered Jessica's reaction to hearing Agent Hamlin's name.

Jessica didn't have time to respond as Boyd stopped to let the women enter the auditorium first.

Charlie nodded thanks and slipped past Boyd. Jessica

also nodded and followed Charlie down the carpeted aisle to the second row of metal and cloth theatre chairs. The red cloth seats looked about thirty years old, and the room smelled a bit like tar and mortar. Charlie wrinkled her nose as she sank down into the crusty stadium seat. Her cream-colored pencil skirt was not going to like this fabric. She rotated onto her left hip and readjusted the catchy material.

"How about lunch after the ceremony, Agent Winslow?"

Charlie glanced up to see Greg standing a row ahead of her, smiling with all his perfect teeth showing.

"Give us a quick chance to get to know each other before we're stuck together," Greg offered, spreading his hands open.

Charlie stood up and her chair seat swung shut with rusty growl. She straightened her blazer.

"We have a long drive back to Albany, and probably shouldn't delay too long," Charlie replied. She didn't want to stay any longer than she had to around this man.

I've got to untangle why he bothers me, Charlie noted.

"That works for me, something quick it is. Agent Boyd, Ma'am Handler, will you join us, as well?" Greg glanced at

Jessica and his smile changed to a boyish grin. Charlie could feel Boyd roll his eyes.

Charlie glanced over at Jessica who was a little flushed.

Is she going to fall for this...frat boy?

"Yes, we will meet you in the atrium after," Boyd finished. He sat down with a grunt, ending the conversation. Boyd looked over at Jessica with a glare. She shrugged in apology and sat up a little straighter. Boyd looked away and Jessica jokingly fanned her face. Charlie smiled back but this time the smile didn't reach her eyes.

It's wrong. Everything is wrong.

7

Long Nights

I OPEN MY eyes. Nothing. Blackness. I can't breathe! Gasping for air, I realize I'm lying on my back, buried in sand. The sand is crushing my chest; I'm sinking into the earth beneath me. My body feels heavy, so heavy. Sand fills my mouth, ears, throat. My chest burns, my lungs beg for air. Every inhale feels like ravenous fire ants have been unleashed on my internal flesh.

A hand pushes through the sand, reaches for me. I try to reach out, but my hand is limp by my side, pinned down by the weight of the sand. The hand reaches one final time, fingers stretching out, then disappears.

"Charlie!" A voice calls and fades away. "Charlie.

Remember me!" The voice, it's so familiar, so kind.

I'm sitting now in a never-ending hallway leaning against a door. The carpet is worn, blue. I feel safe, warm. But the voices are getting angry. They're yelling.

I hear a door open; a metal holiday bell jingles against the wood. I'm standing now. The air goes black.

I suddenly feel afraid, alone. I clench my fist. The carpet fades to stained, broken tile. I am sweating, cold beadlets run down my back. I begin to shiver. In fear or it's cold in this pitch-black space.

I scream as Mother appears in the darkness. In her raised hand, scissors glint, freshly sharpened. Mother swipes at me with the scissors, catching my sleeve and then yanks back, ripping the seams. I try to run away, but I can't move. I'm paralyzed. My legs are iron posts, welded to the floor.

I worry about fixing my torn shirt. Mother will punish me if I don't fix the shirt! I am panicking.

But I can't find my sewing needle. I've dropped it. I am panting, gasping for life. I am dying without oxygen; my lungs collapsing in on themselves. Fire spreads through my chest.

Mother dives at me again, this time plunging the scissors deep in my heart. I scream in agony. She pulls back again and disappears in a fog of air.

"Help me, help me, help me," I whimper as I desperately try to pin my heart closed to stop the bleeding.

8

On the Road

CHARLIE WOKE IN pain, her alarm clock beeping rudely from the nightstand. She gingerly reached out and slapped the top of the wooden-framed clock to silence it; the red lines read 5:30 AM. The nightmare still hanging in the air, Charlie pushed the blankets off and moved her legs to the floor. She was drenched in sweat and desperately needed a naproxen to calm the inflammation in her rib cage.

With sheer will, she got out of bed and walked across the room to the ensuite bathroom. She glanced up at the mirror as she entered and gasped, her mother stared back at her from the other side of the mirror. Charlie shook her head and blinked hard, begging the nightmare to go away. Opening her eyes she looked back at the mirror, only seeing her own reflection. She'd never noticed how much she took after her mom until now.

Everybody always said Mother was gorgeous, and Charlie agreed on the outside, Patricia was stunning. Reddish-brown hair. Her tight curls perfectly sculpted. Emerald eyes classically lined with a wing of black liquid. A perfect hourglass shape standing at 5'5". But Charlie knew beneath all that pretty was the real Patricia. The hate, the bitterness, and the abuse.

Charlie rarely took the time to properly care for her curls, and generally kept her hair twisted up on the top of her head. Makeup was not part of Charlie's routine, either, although she had the same emerald eyes. She took after her mom in shape but stood a couple inches taller. She worked out regularly and was well-toned whereas Mother, although narrow, was soft.

Mom always looked haggard and over tired. Guess that's why I look like her right now. I'm overdone, tired, and angry.

After the answering machine message from her mother,

she'd cried for hours. She hated her mother, and yet she'd had the nerve to apologize on her death bed and make Charlie feel guilty for avoiding her. Later that night, after too much red wine, Charlie had placed a bouquet of lilies on the table, cut fresh from her garden. While she didn't know her mom's favorite flower, she figured it was something to say goodbye. But in reality, she still felt numb to her passing...after all, she'd been dead to Charlie for a decade.

The image of Mother throwing scissors shifted across her vision again and Charlie shivered. The reoccurring nightmare had only gotten worse since the case with Hen and her hospital stay. She'd lost a lot of sleep to the jingling bell.

Charlie stepped away from the mirror and her mom's reflection. She pushed the image of her nightmare away and told herself it was time to focus on work. No time for the past. Despite her irritation at the no-contact case, Charlie was anxious to get back to work.

One hour later, freshly showered, packed, and rib inflammation under control, Charlie said goodbye to her house, sank into the VW, and headed toward the field office in Albany.

The drive to Albany was curvy, the leaves beginning their descent into the fall red that Charlie loved so much. As she pulled into the mechanic's parking lot, Robbie approached her.

"Hi Robbie. I'm probably just being picky, but this is the second time it's done this. Maybe it's time for a new transmission?" Charlie said as she stepped out of the Rabbit.

"Or maybe you need lessons on how to drive properly. I've seen you ride second like it's a motorbike," Robbie laughed. Then sobering, he said, "I will take good care of her, as always."

Robbie cared deeply about cars, as if they were his children. He'd taken care of Charlie's Rabbit for ten of the fifteen years of its life. Despite his mechanic shop looking like a flea market of car parts, empty soda cans, and cardboard boxes, he knew where every tool and part resided.

"I know you always do," Charlie said firmly. "She's just shifting hard at third gear again, sometimes I feel like she just flat out misses the gear."

Robbie's dead stare in response made Charlie chuckle. Robbie was a Volkswagen expert and likely already knew exactly what the Rabbit needed just by smelling the tailpipe. Charlie always suspected Robbie hoped one day she'd sell him the Rabbit—he clearly loved the car as much as she did.

"Okay, okay. I'm leaving," Charlie said putting her hands up in surrender. "Please call Jessica if you need me." Charlie handed Robbie her phone number and gestured across the street at her building. "I'll be back in a few weeks. You sure you don't mind storing her for that time?"

"I've got you covered. I'll check her from nose to tailpipe and let you know if I find anything else," Robbie said with a short nod. He grabbed the phone number and keys from Charlie's outstretched hand and headed towards the VW.

"I checked the odometer, Robbie!" Charlie called after him with a laugh.

"Yeah, yeah, no road trips. I know," Robbie called over his shoulder with feigned disappointment.

Charlie watched him walk away as Robbie mumbled something about rolling the odometer back. She smiled but felt sad about leaving her car behind. The motel she'd call home for a few weeks was in Mulrose, Pennsylvania, deep in the Susquehanna Valley. She knew the three-hour drive from Albany to Mulrose would be full of leafy, twisted, quiet roads and she desperately wanted her Rabbit for the drive. She smiled imagining Boyd's reaction if she showed up with her Rabbit again.

Looking away from the car with a sigh, she grabbed her hand-woven duffle and leather briefcase, walked to the crosswalk on McCarty Ave, and made her way to the office to meet Greg.

Greg walked out of the building just as Charlie crossed the parking lot full of black and grey sedans with tinted windows. He had car keys in his right hand and a black leather duffle in his left. His suit was meticulously pressed and perfectly fitted to his broad shoulders. His wavy hair gently ruffled in the breeze as he approached Charlie in the parking lot. *He still looks like he belongs in college fraternity flirting with sorority girls,* Charlie thought shaking her head. *He certainly doesn't look like an FBI agent. Probably why he's successful—nobody suspects.*

"Hey, partner! You look better than last time I saw you. Glad you're up and around." Greg grinned. He lifted the keychain and threaded a pocketknife onto the ring.

"Hi Greg. Yup, I'm good as new. I'm going to go grab my keys from Jessica and I'll see you at the motel in Mulrose."

"Wait, Charlie. We're in that car," Greg said pointing to a black Crown Victoria in parking spot number twenty-seven. "Afraid we have to share this trip. I know how you like your own ride, but apparently there is a shortage today."

"That's weird," Charlie replied, stopping short. "Jessica told me we'd have separate cars like normal." Her grey pencil skirt caught a breeze, and she reached down to flatten the fabric, dropping her duffel bag.

"Ha, you know how fast things change around here, Charlie," Greg shrugged, bending over to gather Charlie's bag.

Charlie reached out for the bag, but Greg popped the trunk and loaded both of their duffel bags.

"How about I drive, and you catch me up on your thoughts with the case?" Greg said closing the trunk.

Charlie hesitated, looking around at the parking lot full of cars.

I always get my own car. She glanced up at the brown building and the window where she knew Jessica sat then across the street where Robbie was pulling her Rabbit into the garage. One of her requirements of employment was she drove to cases alone. As undercover agents, this tactic was necessary. Charlie went in undercover then Greg showed up with the calvary when Charlie alerted him she had the information or person they needed.

"The town is walkable from what I've heard," Greg offered. "It's been a few weeks since we caught up, wouldn't be the worst use of the drive." Greg smiled then opened the passenger door and gestured inside the car. Charlie knew that smile would make Jessica melt, but it only irritated her.

"Thanks," Charlie mumbled walking to the passenger side and sliding in.

Guess I'll call Jessica when we arrive. See if a porter can bring me a car when it's available.

The drive to Mulrose was as beautiful as Charlie expected. The leaves were beginning to change, and a bright orange menagerie of texture was the backdrop for the drive.

"One thing I can't understand, why did you come early when I was with Hen and his buffoons?" Charlie asked after a few minutes of painful small talk.

Greg chuckled at Charlie's forwardness then sucked in a breath.

"We threw that rescue together so fast, I was concerned you'd gotten in over your head," Greg began tapping the top of the steering wheel.

"Well, that's nice," Charlie shot back crossing her arms. She looked out the passenger window at the trees rushing by.

"Woah, Chariot, hold up. The amount of drugs Karl gave you was not part of the plan, I was worried about you," Greg said glancing at Charlie. Charlie looked over at him and saw he was being sincere. She smiled apologetically and forced herself to take a breath.

"We got a tip that Hen kidnapped two girls instead of just Adtel. That threw off the whole plan. Despite your amazing skills," Greg winked at Charlie, "no way could you rescue two teens in that short of time. Sure enough, we narrow down your location and immediately hear gun shots. I know you're smart, and not likely the one that got shot, so I give you a few minutes longer. Finally, we're set up for infiltration and I smell natural gas. I tell the team it's time to go in when suddenly Hen and his son, Neil, are rushing to their car. We take them down without a fuss, but Hen's nephew, Jones, is nowhere to be seen. We hear another gunshot and a moment later you're being dragged out of the house with a teenager. You were in bad shape, Charlie." Greg stopped talking and gulped back a hiccup. He went silent and stared at the road.

Charlie watched Greg for a moment. He seemed to be fighting back tears and Charlie softened towards him, appreciating his response and kicking herself for being so defensive.

"Thank you, Greg. You made the right call. You came at exactly the right time," Charlie said. "The whole case went sideways from the moment I walked into Johnnie's J. I'm lucky you're my partner and knew when to change our plan without first consulting me."

Charlie smiled at Greg, and he chuckled. He glanced over at her, his emerald eyes shiny.

"Thanks, partner," Greg replied with a soft smile.

After a quick coffee break and naproxen dose in

Oneonta, Charlie pulled the brown case files from her briefcase.

"Alright, let's try to avoid me being drugged this time," Charlie said, and Greg gave a thumbs up. "Case #1185. A tip came in from an undisclosed credible source that Tucker Trucking & Freight of Old Mill, Pennsylvania, engages in illegal international shipping, including narcotics, explosives, and possibly weapons. The owner, James Maynan, is not in ViCAP, the criminal database, nor have there ever been any complaints against the company which has been in operation for about fifteen years or so. This case was originally brought to us two years ago but went into a backlog due to lack of evidence."

Greg snorted. Charlie turned towards him.

"With thousands of cases coming in each year, we don't have time to go after each," Charlie said protectively. "And not many agents agree to a no-contact case, either. Remind me where you were before the Buffalo branch?"

"Baltimore was before Buffalo. When I first met you, I'd only been at Buffalo for a few months, but I received the Shield of Bravery for the Inona Case. Why?"

"Why did you want to leave Buffalo?"

"When Boyd started hunting for your previous partner's replacement, I was happy to apply. The ADIC at Buffalo and I didn't see eye to eye after what happened in Inona. We lost three guys, and I barely made it out myself. Out of my years of service, I'd never seen such a suicidal bloodbath. The tactics were all wrong, the CIRG men, rest in peace, were under-trained and a risk. If I hadn't gotten out of there with the intel I found, we'd also have lost the case. Thanks to me, I not only kept more men from going on the case but also got the bad guy. You never forget the stare of a dead man." Greg wrinkled his nose.

Charlie flinched slightly and turned forward in her seat.

"Ah, hell. I'm sorry, Charlie." Greg smacked the steering wheel then put his hand on Charlie's arm. "You already know that. Tim deserved better. You guys were great together. It's the risk of relationships in our line of work. Tim knew that."

Charlie nodded but pulled her arm away from Greg's warm hand. She fought to clear the image of her fiancé's dead stare and his body sprawled out in the entry way of their townhome and her desperate wish that her mom had still been around to call. Very few moments in her life left her emotional, but that was one topic she avoided at all costs.

"Have there been any leads on his case since we last talked about it? It's been just over two years since it happened, right?" Greg asked moving his hand back to the middle arm rest.

"Yeah, twenty-eight months. No. Not a thing. And now, it's probably backlogged," Charlie replied, looking at him with a small smile, attempting sarcasm. She didn't want to talk about Tim anymore. Didn't have the energy to go into that emotional turmoil. She'd face it later.

Or maybe never, she considered.

Greg smiled, appreciating the humor and understanding her desire to change the subject.

"Looks like this is the motel we get to call home for the next few weeks," Greg said as he pulled up to a rundown motel with rotten wooden trim and sagging porches. The sign on the street claimed each room had a bathtub and cable, but Charlie knew she'd barely be in her room. The motel had a main lobby which then opened into an interior courtyard with the three stories of doors looking down on the dirt space. Charlie imagined at one point the courtyard had been beautiful and lush. Certainly not anymore.

"Lovely," Charlie said looking around. "Do they only have one room available, or do we each get our own?"

Greg laughed as he put the car in park then walked around to the back of the car to gather the duffel bags.

Charlie stepped out of the car and put her hands on top of the car.

"Hey, did you study the maps before we left or something? How'd you know where we were going?" Charlie leaned forward and stared at Greg. He glanced behind him at a passing car then back at Charlie.

"Yeah, of course. I knew you'd be busy reading the case files so didn't want to keep your hands busy with maps. Besides, in case you didn't notice, it was like three turns," Greg responded with a shrug.

Charlie brushed a leaf off the top of the car and made a noise of agreement. Greg seemed distracted and inside his head. His shoulders were tense, his lips a straight line.

Maybe he still feels bad about his comment regarding dead men.

Charlie turned away from Greg and glanced down the

street at the quaint, albeit aged town. The hotel was near the end of the main part of town. And as Greg promised, the town appeared walkable.

"Oh hey, we didn't talk about our cover names, yet. I'll be Jane Blander. Who do you want to be?" Charlie asked.

Greg glanced up at the sky and rubbed his chin. He raked his fingers through his curls then took a breath.

"How about Paul Merchant?" Greg finally said.

"Like Doctor Merchant? From that foreign horror film about bloodlines or something?" Charlie laughed.

"What? It's a perfectly good name!" Greg said seriously.

"Fine, that works. But I won't be calling you doctor, that movie scared the hell out of me," Charlie said.

"Fair," Greg responded walking towards the lobby.

Charlie was beginning to feel the rush of the start of a new case; a buoyancy flew through her like the fall breeze encircling the October Glory maples surrounding the parking lot. Excitement flooded her veins.

Despite her initial hesitations, she felt this case was going to be a real thriller.

9

Unexpected Moments

AFTER DISCUSSING THE case further with Greg in the abandoned motel courtyard, Charlie expressed her desire to rest. She also wanted time to further digest the case information in the brown files. They both agreed on a late lunch/early dinner, where they'd finalize their plan of attack and divvy up the responsibilities.

Still riding the high of the excitement of a new case, Charlie took the time to apply light makeup and attempted to refresh her long curls, opting to leave them down for once. Styling curly hair in a motel bathroom was a part of the job Charlie didn't particularly enjoy. She could only pack so many hair products in a small duffel. She leaned forward and dabbed her lips one last time, favoring the way her hair turned out after being up in a scrunchie all morning.

The lip gloss slipped from her fingers and Charlie bent down to retrieve the bottle from under the cabinet. Straightening up, Charlie glanced in the mirror and sucked in a breath.

The image of Mother from her nightmare stared back at Charlie from the mirror, inches from her face. Cold dark eyes pleaded at Charlie. A boney hand reached out and clawed at the air.

Charlie screamed and jumped back, a chill ran up her arms and across her shoulders.

Remember, Charlie, remember.

Heavy words echoed through the bathroom and shook the shower curtain.

Charlie put her hands over her ears and ran out of the bathroom, slamming the door behind her.

No, no, no, no. Charlie sat on the bed and squeezed her eyes shut. *Leave me alone, go away.*

After a few more moments, Charlie finally opened her eyes and put her hands in her lap. The room was full of sun streaming in through the white curtains. The bedspread was decorated with yellow sunflowers and a yellow armchair sat cheerily in the corner. She glanced down at her hands and willed them to stop shaking.

These nightmares have got to stop!

Still feeling a little shaken, Charlie took a deep breath and willed herself forward. She dressed in a silky multi-colored blouse and dark jeans that hugged her hips then swapped last minute for a light blue V-neck sweater and looser light jeans that felt more reasonable for the aged feeling of the town. Locking her issued Glock in the room safe, she decided she was ready.

At precisely four, Charlie reentered the motel lobby where Greg was already waiting in a tall-backed wooden chair. He glanced up briefly from his newspaper as she entered the room then realizing it was her, put down his newspaper and smiled.

"Charlie, you look refreshed and beautiful. I feel a little underdressed now," Greg said playfully, looking down at his clothes.

Charlie didn't try to hide her eye roll but smiled at his feigned discomfort. Greg was anything but underdressed.

He wore tan colored pants that accented his strong legs and a blue pinstripe collared shirt with the sleeves rolled up to just below his elbow. His curls were brushed off his forehead and perfectly coiled as always. Charlie considered if she'd ever seen his hair out of place.

"Thank you, but I'm pretty sure every wave on your hair is perfectly structured, that makes you classier than me," Charlie replied.

"Ha, my hair does its own thing," Greg said laughing. "But thanks." He patted his hair gently and scratched the back of his neck.

"Shall we walk? I think the restaurant is about two blocks. It's nice outside for this time of year," Greg said walking towards the front door of the lobby.

"Sure, lead the way," Charlie said.

The hinges on the front door of the motel squealed as Greg pulled on the handle and held it open for Charlie to pass through.

Gentle early October breezes swirled leaves around Greg and Charlie's feet as they walked towards the restaurant in silence. The sun touched the peak of the distant hills, casting long shadows on the buildings and across the streets as they neared the first crosswalk. The trees gripped hard to their orange leaves, swaying silently in the wind. Charlie took a deep breath to savor the fresh fall scent in the air.

"Oliver!" A woman's shrill scream bounced through the air breaking the serene moment. Charlie glanced down the street to the left and saw a barefoot woman clenching an infant tight to her chest. She was running full speed after a little boy who clearly decided that the middle of the street was his racetrack. The toddler had a large head start on the mother despite her pace. He glanced back briefly at his mother, giggled boyishly, then continued his jog down the street.

"Oliver! Stop!" The mother yelled grasping tighter to the infant, trying to protect her tiny head from bouncing. Tears were streaming down her face as she leaned forward to quicken her speed.

Even though the town was small, the main road was a thoroughfare from other local towns. Vacationers drove fast and distracted, worrying about their next whiskey, or if they'd packed their skis. The child was running directly towards the main intersection of the town, completely oblivious to the danger. Charlie and Greg were close to the intersection.

Before Charlie could react, Greg was running towards the child.

"Stop traffic that way and I'll get the kid!" Greg yelled back at Charlie pointing at the oncoming cars.

Charlie ran to the crosswalk on the opposite side of the intersection. Hurtling into the street, Charlie waved her arms and yelled at drivers to stop.

Horns honked, brakes squealed, drivers yelled, and the mother screamed.

Then silence.

Still standing in the middle of the intersection, Charlie put her arms down. Afraid to look, she forced herself to turn towards Greg's direction. Greg was standing by the grill of an Oldsmobile sedan with his back to Charlie. His back showed heavy breathing. His shoulders lifted and sagged down.

The mother, still holding her infant, stood a few feet away, panting, crying, unable to move.

"No," Charlie breathed as she ran towards Greg. She reached Greg as he turned around. In his arms, a scared, but unharmed, toddler squirmed to be let down. Charlie put her hands over her mouth to trap a sob of relief. Children were rarely part of her cases, and she felt an urge to cry and cuddle the child.

"Momma, momma," the little boy murmured, close to crying and uncertain about the stranger who was holding him tightly. His sandy brown hair stuck straight up, his dark eyelashes framed perfect ocean blue eyes.

"Oliver, you naughty boy," the boy's mom said in a hesitated whisper. She approached Greg, tears rolling down her face.

"Sir, thank you. Thank you. If you hadn't been here..." She glanced around at the sedan and the busy intersection. She sobbed and took a deep breath to settle her heart. "He got out when I was making a bottle. He's a curious little man. Here, can you hold her for a moment?" The mother reached the infant out towards Charlie, her face somber.

Charlie looked up at Greg who still clung to the wiggling toddler then back at the distraught mother.

"Yeah, uh, sure. Of course."

Charlie gathered the infant from the woman's arms and

set her against her chest and cradled her with her left arm.

The mother reached out for the toddler in Greg's arm and walked him over to the sidewalk, bending down to his face level.

Charlie looked down at the featherweight human in her arms. The infant girl had wispy black hair and light skin. She was tightly swaddled in a soft pink blanket that only showed her round cheeks and the top of her head. Charlie touched the baby's hair gently. The infant yawned then opened her eyelids and stared back at Charlie with dark green eyes.

"I had a dream about our daughter last night," Tim said barely above a whisper. He and Charlie were sprawled out in bed, the satin sheets draped across their naked bodies. The pillows somewhere on the floor. It was well after midnight. The wine bottle was empty, and the lights were off. He ran his fingers across her bare shoulder.

Charlie smiled and closed her eyes. "Mmhm. What was she like?"

"She had your curls, and emerald eyes...

like you. Soft porcelain skin. These rosy cheeks that I instantly wanted to pinch. When she smiled at me, I felt like I'd seen an ancient Egyptian princess. Like God decided I deserved another precious life to love. She was so perfect." Tim reached out and played with a curl by Charlie's forehead. *"She was so real, Char. Whenever you're ready, let's find out what she'd look like in real life...."*

The driver of the Oldsmobile honked at the pedestrians in the middle of the street, completely unaware of the almost tragedy. Greg gave a sharp wave as a sarcastic apology and grabbed Charlie's elbow to direct her to the sidewalk. Charlie shook her head to clear the memory and brushed a tear from her cheek. The infant closed her eyes again and fell asleep. Charlie felt comforted by the little heater buried in her arms.

"Oliver, you are not allowed to go outside without mommy or daddy. Ever. Do you understand?" The mother said sternly. The toddler nodded empathetically, wiping snot away with the sleeve of his shirt. She grabbed the toddler in a tight hug and pushed his hair out his face. The toddler squirmed and asked to be put down. Charlie glanced down again at the sleeping infant and brushed soft black wisps off her forehead.

The mother sighed and put the toddler down on the sidewalk, grasping his hand tightly. She looked at Charlie and Greg. "Kids are so innocent to danger. Thank you again, so much. I'm Debra. This is Oliver. And the newborn is Rosie."

"I'm Jane and this is Paul," Charlie replied with a smile.

"Do you all live here?" Debra asked.

"No, we're here on a journal assignment. We both work for a travel magazine. We're doing an article on local businesses and how they operate," Greg said.

"That's lucky for our town! I work at Tina's Cafe over on Lincoln during the weekday mornings. Come by anytime and breakfast is on me. I can give you whatever quotes you need."

"Thanks, I'd like that," Charlie said staring at the infant. The little girl was dreaming and her lips twitched and puckered. Charlie thought the child was the most beautiful thing she'd ever seen.

Debra smiled and retrieved the infant, thanking Charlie for holding Rosie. She grabbed Oliver's hand tightly and turned, retracing the steps she'd ran along chasing after her toddler.

"Greg... that was incredible," Charlie said, watching Debra walk away with her children, the toddler already trying to get out of his mother's firm grasp. Charlie's arms felt empty and cold.

"We risk our lives every day in this job, Charlie," Greg said somberly. "Just glad we were here." He watched the family safely enter a building further down the street then said, "Let's get moving."

Charlie stood for one more moment then followed Greg as he entered the crosswalk.

"You looked like a natural with the baby in your arms, Charlie. Seemed to even like it once you got over the shock of being handed an infant," Greg said as he stepped on the sidewalk. He smiled over at Charlie and touched her shoulder.

"I'm not sure I've ever held a baby before, honestly. I was terrified I'd drop her," Charlie replied. She felt her adrenaline subsiding and again focused on the fresh air and observing the new town.

The sidewalk faded into an aged slatted wooden walkway under a wooden awning. Several shops with glass displays advertised everything from rare books to a whiskey bar. Despite the run-down feeling of the main street, Charlie saw several shops she'd be happy to wander through. A Tiffany lamp caught her eye, and she stopped to admire the green and blue glasswork amongst the brass base.

"Wow, we might have to go to plan B, Char," Greg said, distracting Charlie. She glanced over and he pointed out their destination at the end of the wooden porch.

The shimmering restaurant sign illuminated several cars circling the already over-filled parking lot. Swarms of people milled around the entrance.

"Glad we walked," Charlie said, trying to sound lighthearted. "Although that doesn't help us with that crowd. And apparently even you are underdressed, Greg."

Charlie laughed as she noticed all the people were in evening wear. And they were flooding in from everywhere—the parking lot, from down the street, from around the corner.

"What is going on here?" Greg asked as he picked up his pace. "We'll check in with the hostess but likely going somewhere else."

"Agreed. Excuse me," Charlie said as she tried to pass through the crowd. Nobody moved or made room, so Charlie had to move left and right to get through the mass. Finally reaching the front door, Greg reached around Charlie and opened the door as she hurried in. She noticed that despite the amount of people milling around, most of the tables inside were empty. Greg and Charlie glanced at each other in confusion.

"Yes, sir?" The hostess said tiredly, eying the crowd outside.

"Table for two?" Greg asked, feeling like he already knew the answer.

"I'm sorry, we're closed for a private party," she said with a sigh. She put both her hands on the stand in front of her as if to brace herself. "We open to the general public again tomorrow at 4:00 PM."

"Ah, that explains the evening gowns and tuxedos," Greg said.

The waitress guffawed. Then cleared her throat.

"If you're needing food tonight, the closest option is Genter's Dance Hall. They're one block north." The hostess looked up behind Greg and Charlie at a woman dressed in more shiny jewelry than silk fabric. "Ma'am, no, not yet, please." To Charlie and Greg, "Excuse me, and sorry."

Greg gently grabbed Charlie's elbow and directed her to the door.

"I feel sorry for that hostess," Charlie said watching the young woman gracefully sweep across the floor and brush past the exasperated hostess. "This looks like a challenging group of people. And how much would that cost to rent out a whole restaurant? Also, a dance hall? For dinner?"

"I agree on all topics, but I'm hungry," Greg said. He looked up and down the street with high heels clicking in every direction around him as Charlie huddled nearby. "Doesn't seem like we have a choice, and I can guarantee none of these people will be there. That's a win in my book."

A man and woman approached Greg and Charlie and cut right between them with no apology. An elbow pierced Charlie's forearm.

"Okay, you win," Charlie said looking back at the couple in shock. "What is with people?"

Greg shook his head in reply and crossed the street. As he reached the curb, he jumped and kicked his heels in the air, then turned north.

Charlie laughed at Greg's maneuver as they walked past the restaurant on the other side of the road. The hostess must have given up because the throng of people were now pushing their way through the bottleneck of the front doors.

Charlie could hear their destination before she could see it. Country music wasn't her genre of choice, but she recognized Brooks & Dunn echoing down the street and felt the boots stomping in her chest.

Despite a decent crowd, Charlie and Greg felt more comfortable than their other attempt. They opted for a spot at the bar that overlooked the dance floor. The music was good, and the bartender was quick to take their order. After a few minutes, they both relaxed.

Charlie chose a beer and a cheeseburger with fries. She'd told Greg it was classic bar food and hard to mess up. Greg followed her lead and ordered the same. They ate in silence and watched the dancers laugh in lines, periodically stomping their feet along with a beat they recognized. After several songs and group dances, a popular song ended. The band said they would be back after a short break and the dance floor emptied.

"I think it's easily been ten years since I last visited a dance hall," Charlie admitted as she munched on her dwindling leftover fries. She watched several twenty-somethings walk to their seats as if they'd just woken up from a nap completely refreshed, despite dancing several songs in a row. "I used to love it, but now it just makes me feel old."

"Charlie, do you think any of these women could do half of what you do in the field? You've got a mean right hook, and you fight like a scrappy prison girl," Greg said leaning back. "You nearly died and were doing a full workout two weeks later." He took a long sip of an amber beer, his eyes smiling at her over the frothy glass.

"Thank you, I think?" Charlie laughed. "I tried to do burpees at the hospital and passed out. My nurse wouldn't leave me alone after that."

"You did not," Greg said laughing from his stomach.

"That's Charlie. Nobody can keep her down."

Charlie smiled at the compliment and searched his face. She was relieved to see that despite his teasing, Greg seemed sincere. His lips were slightly parted in a full smile; his emerald eyes shone in the spotlight refractions.

He really is handsome, Charlie admitted.

"How about one dance before we go, Charlie?" Greg asked, his eyes intense.

Charlie realized he'd been watching her observe him and felt goosebumps raise on her arms. She blushed.

"The band isn't even playing right now," Charlie said, relieved at the excuse. "Otherwise, I would."

As if on cue, the band returned and began to play "Time Marches On" by Tracy Lawrence. The lurking notes drifted through the hall. Couples returned to the dance floor and danced close with their partners.

"Your lucky day, then," Greg said. He stepped off the bar stool and reached his right hand out to Charlie.

Charlie hesitated. She'd always easily resisted Greg's charms. Often found his passes annoying. Even easier was her rule that she didn't date coworkers. But tonight, she felt less resistant. Her insides weren't screaming to get away from him. She'd always assumed that feeling was because of her rules and his charm.

What is one dance, anyways? She reasoned in a moment of lapsed judgement. *Besides, we're undercover. We have to look like we are writers, not stiff FBI agents.*

Placing her hand in Greg's, she slid off the stool and allowed him to lead her to the dance floor. She tried not to react when he turned her in a full circle and stopped her, pulling her chest to chest. He dropped his arm down her back and settled it along the narrow of her waist.

Uh-oh, she thought, as she felt his closeness, his strength. His arm tightened around her, closing any gap between them. He swayed them both on tempo for a few moments then deftly directed her into a few dance steps. She was impressed with his lead and grateful she knew how to accurately respond. After a few more steps and turns, she noticed she was grinning. She looked at him and saw that he, too, was smiling.

I could get lost in those eyes tonight, Charlie caught herself thinking. *No, no, no. You cannot. Stop grinning like a schoolgirl.*

Greg brought Charlie in for one last close sway, placing

both their hands against his shoulder. He pressed her gently closer. Charlie felt herself leaning into his chest as the slow song finally came to an end snapping Charlie back to reality.

Grateful the internal argument could be over, Charlie turned to exit the dance floor as the band transitioned into an upbeat line dance. Greg grabbed her hand and pointed to the forming line with a pleading expression. Charlie rolled her eyes but decided, in her abandoned state, it was better to take a breather before walking back to the motel alone with Greg. Charlie slipped between two brunettes with cropped jean shorts and shiny boots hoping to stay a person away from Greg. Instead, he squeezed in next to her and grabbed her hand. Pulling her to the left to follow the other dancers, Greg stayed right on step. Charlie could see the petite brunettes drooling over Greg, but realized they were eying her, too.

He's all yours, girls, Charlie thought, looking longingly at the exit.

Greg caught her eye as if sensing her discomfort and gave her an apologetic grin and shrugged his shoulders.

Charlie suddenly felt a flush of selfishness. Greg had never given her a reason to be on guard. His flirting was always above the line, and he'd never made a move on her. All he'd ever done was encourage her and protect her, even when she didn't think she needed protection. Who was she to ruin his fun with her uncertainties?

Charlie smiled back at Greg and enthusiastically dipped her shoulder into the next kick and step. Greg smiled warmly and laughed out loud. Before she knew it, he'd grabbed both her hands and spun her out of the line into a fast two step. Charlie forced herself to focus on her steps and his lead, enjoying the symmetry of their moves. Within moments the line had ceased and instead formed a circle around Greg and Charlie. Greg pushed Charlie into a complex mix of steps, ducking, pretzels, kicks, and bows, both keeping time and flowing as if rehearsed. As the song end, the crowd hollered and clapped, some even patted them on the back.

"Thank you to our dancers for filling the floor. You available next week, too?" The band quipped into the mic.

Charlie waved them away and laughed, still holding Greg's hand. She was out of breath but pleased with herself and equally impressed with Greg. He was a great lead, which made her side of the dance easier.

"That was way more fun than I'd expected, Greg. You were right," Charlie admitted as they paid their bill and walked to the door. A cold rush of air pushed through them as they stepped outside. "Wow, the temperature has dropped. Didn't know we'd be gone so long," she said, laughing again—a lighthearted sound she didn't know she could make.

Greg put his arm around her shoulders lightly and said close to her ear, "Thanks for going along with it. You were excellent in there." He gently squeezed her shoulder.

"I must admit, I am impressed with your dancing skills. Not many men can do what you did, and you never once stomped on my feet!"

"You know, you're a great partner in more ways than one. You didn't miss one cue."

"Good thing, because those brunettes would have trampled me for a turn with you."

"Ha, I didn't notice. I only had my eyes on one woman," Greg said quietly.

Charlie was hyper aware of the warmth Greg's body

emanated. The feel of his arm over her shoulders coursed through her. He was quiet, introverted. They walked the rest of the way in silence but stayed close. Charlie glanced at him then looked away. He was looking at her, too.

Maybe he's just cold, Charlie thought, trying to focus on her footsteps.

At the entrance to the hotel, Greg paused. Charlie looked up at his face, his arm still around her shoulders. Greg looked down at her with a stern but soft expression. His eyes glowed a haunting green under the bare light bulb.

"We are always chasing the bad guys, Charlie. Always focused on not dying. Had fun with you, tonight. The restaurant being closed was the best thing that ever happened. It was nice to see you relax. You lit up that dance floor with your smile...wow." Greg turned Charlie towards him, smiling. "I know it's been hard since Tim died, but there's so much more out there that you don't even know about yet."

Greg leaned in close to her face. Charlie sucked in a breath debating her next move. She felt confused, uncertain. He kissed her cheek and lingered for a moment.

Pulling back, he gave her shoulders one final squeeze. Opening the squeaky motel door, he disappeared into the lobby.

10

Pulling at the Thread

THE NEXT SEVERAL days rolled by in a blur. Charlie spent most of her time at Old Mill Courthouse going through decades of tax records, newspaper articles, building permits, government contracts, and small claim reports. Tucker Trucking & Freight appeared to be a well-respected, well-represented, small-town business. Newspaper articles talked about the various sponsorships and donations the company provided to support local activities. Pictures of the warehouse were common, but no photographs of the owners. Tax records showed no deficits or back taxes. There was only one building permit filed in the last sixty years...what appeared to be a rebuilding of some damage from a corner of the warehouse. The current owner took over at a young age due to his father's death. Charlie found an article written fifteen years ago talking fondly of the man named Peter and his son, James, and the great life Peter led until he died from cancer "too young."

The building permit was the only piece of information that was different from her file from the field office. The information in the brown folders said the company was about fifteen years old, whereas that permit was filed thirty years ago.

Not helpful, Charlie mused, *but always good to clear up datasets. For all we know, this illegal stuff was happening decades ago.*

Greg had been doing the footwork, driving to neighboring towns and asking around. Charlie skimmed his notes periodically but hadn't found anything useful. Greg had great recall and generally stored information in his head. He once told Charlie that before he started working with her, he never wrote anything down, because it could later be incriminating. Now he logs *some* things for Charlie.

And useless notes, at that, she mused.

Between the two of them, and from a paper trail perspective, nothing had been found yet to incriminate the warehouse. Charlie was beginning to get irritable. She wasn't used to this much down time, and usually Jessica did the research. She returned the folders to the clerk and thanked her for the time.

Charlie left the courthouse and walked towards Tina's Cafe to meet Greg for a late lunch. They'd settled into their disguise of a couple of writers doing research for a magazine about businesses that keep small towns alive. Still grateful to Greg for saving her son, Debra considered Greg and Charlie regulars and happily answered any questions they asked. So far, they hadn't mentioned Tucker Trucking, but after another disappointing day at the courthouse, Charlie decided it was time to press in a little harder.

Tina's Cafe was located on Lincoln Avenue, in the heart of the town's downtown district—a line of storefronts that opened into a wood slat walkway and wooden overhangs. The town reminded Charlie of Virginia City, Nevada. Many storefronts had updated their displays to a more modern look, but a few here and there had fallen behind. Overhangs sagged between the supports and black seams of rot heavily dotted the rooflines.

The cafe was somewhere in the middle of updates. The place was clean, but the design was reminiscent of a soda cafe where the waitresses wore skates. A few red booths hung out in the corners with white and red checkered tables in the middle of the room. A red bar with stools lined the wall where a half wall hid the kitchen. The walls in the dining room were covered with photographs, some recent, while others were black and white with well-loved corners. Charlie loved looking at the photographs and imagining what each of those humans meant to the cafe.

Greg waved from the corner booth as she approached. Charlie felt her stomach flip flop as she slid into the red seat across from him. She knew to avoid the corner edge of the table where a metal piece was fraying. The first time she'd sat here, she's scratched her fingertip on it. Greg had pulled out his pocketknife in an attempt to lay the metal back in place but with no luck.

"Nothing. Absolutely nothing," Charlie said, shaking her head in frustration, trying to ignore her body's confusing reaction to seeing Greg. "Credible source or not, I can't find anything in the paper trail. Did you have better luck?"

"I sat outside and watched the warehouse for four hours today. I was hoping to see an Italian mobster walk out, but no luck," Greg said with a grin.

"No case is ever that easy," Charlie said rolling her eyes with a laugh. Despite Greg's lighthearted humor, she felt he was feeling a bit of frustration; or perhaps he was restless from his surveillance earlier. She wasn't sure which. They also hadn't talked about dancing, or the almost-kiss outside the motel. Charlie wondered if he wished he'd kissed her, or if he was relieved he didn't. Charlie still didn't know how she felt.

Charlie messed with her ponytail, wishing she'd packed more curl cream. Her hair was frizzy and with the constant wind, she'd had her hair up everyday. She felt a slight headache coming on and loosened the band around the waves. She must have tugged too hard because the rubber band popped and her hair spilled down over her shoulders. She blushed.

"Today was the fifth day I've watched but I haven't seen any patterns yet," Greg said, oblivious to Charlie's snafu.

"Just need one or two people that I can question, but it seems to be mostly drivers and the main employees that come and go. I don't want to spook anybody. No outsiders yet. It'll happen."

Charlie used her fingers to comb the curls off her face. Greg noticed her hair and gawked, all humor removed.

"I know, it's crazy right now," Charlie said, desperately trying to tame her hair.

"Oh, no. Sorry. I just don't think I've seen your hair down much. The curls are great, really," Greg said, his expression neutral. He seemed to be deep in thought.

What is going through his mind? What a weird mood shift.

"Look, I know we agreed to let you do the surveillance and me the sitting around boring healing stuff, but maybe we should switch just one day? Maybe we'll each see something the other didn't?" Charlie said. Greg opened his mouth to respond, when Debra appeared with a notepad. She wore a red linen dress with a checkered apron around her waist. Her blonde hair was in a sleek ponytail, and her eyelids had a sky-blue dusting of eyeshadow.

"Hey guys! Good to see you," Debra said. "How is the

research going today?"

"It's been a rough stretch, not going to lie," Charlie sighed. She glanced over at Greg with an apologetic look. He looked at her curiously, shaking his head. Glancing back at Debra, Charlie said, "I think the next company I'm going to inquire at is a trucking company. Tucker Trucking or something like that?"

Greg straightened in his seat and stared at Charlie with a dark look. She could feel his eyes on her and shivered.

Why is he so possessive over that task? Certainly, sitting in a car is easier than gathering documents from filing cabinets and reading microfiche!

"Yeah, yeah. That's a town over. Been there forever. My dad told me once that some sad accident happened there about thirty years ago or so. Almost closed them down. But the guy that runs it now is brilliant...and not so bad looking, either," Debra said with a smile. She winked at Charlie.

Charlie smiled back briefly. Greg hadn't stopped glaring at Charlie since she asked the question. She shifted in her seat uncomfortably.

"Oh my goodness!" Debra exclaimed looking at Charlie.

"I've never seen your hair down before—it's beautiful! You look a lot like a girl that used to work here years ago. You know, there's probably a picture of her on these walls somewhere..."

"We will take our lunch to-go today. We're kind of in a hurry," Greg interjected. Charlie glanced at Greg with a surprised look. Debra's smile wilted slightly at his tone but nodded and walked off to update the order.

"What was that, Charlie?" Greg said in a low, stern voice after the waitress was out of ear shot. "We agreed to lay low, not go telling everybody that we're interested in a random trucking company a town over!"

"We've been here two weeks and have less information than when we began! Nothing wrong with diving in a little deeper. And did you really have to be rude to her?" Charlie met his eye, her chin up. She felt an impulse to leave as her stomach clenched again. To go back home. End this case. She shivered.

Run.

"Everybody knows everybody in small towns. You never know who you're talking to. No more talk about Tucker Trucking here, got it?" Greg's eyes bore into Charlie. He sat rigid. She couldn't see his hands but imagined they were balled into a tight fist in his lap. She nodded.

"I'm not even hungry. I got a tip I need to follow up on. Catch you at the motel later?" Greg didn't wait for an answer. He got up and stormed across the diner and out the door, letting it slam behind him. Charlie stared after him, unnerved by the outburst. She looked away as Debra approached.

"Sorry about that. Not sure what's up with him today," Charlie said apologetically. "Don't bother ordering his food, I guess."

"No worries. We all have bad days."

Debra glanced over her shoulder at the front door, then turned and leaned closer to Charlie. "Look, I don't want to be rude or ungrateful...he saved my kid after all...and I hardly know you, but there's something about him. I can't tell you what but be careful. Look out for yourself, okay?"

Pausing briefly, Charlie smiled and nodded.

"Well, now that this nonsense is out of the way, why don't you try something new today? I haven't entered your order yet," Debra said. "And move over to the barstools so I can see the rest of the restaurant and the kitchen."

Charlie moved from the corner booth, careful to avoid the sharp edge. She perched on the barstool and leaned on the red bar top.

"Well, what's *your* favorite thing on the menu?" Charlie asked Debra. No other patrons were present, so Debra sat down with Charlie to enjoy a chipped mug of coffee. Charlie wanted to complain to Debra about her lack of information about the trucking company, but Debra still believed Charlie was Jane from Idaho—a magazine writer that was interested in the small town of Mulrose. Nonetheless, Charlie enjoyed the banter with Debra that had become a daily routine. Charlie realized she was starting to miss Jessica.

"I like the parmesan chicken wrap, but our cook created the menu herself and it's all good. We may be a tiny diner in the middle of nowhere, but our owner, Tina, takes pride in sourcing quality foods and our chef, Lisa, loves working with the kitchen staff. Together they only put the good stuff on the menu and let the five-star reviews roll in. It's a win/win," Debra said with a proud smile.

Both women looked behind them as the door opened and a patron stepped in. Charlie noted the newcomer's height—about six-foot-two. He wore his hair curly and piled on top of his head in a perfectly construed messy pile. And his shoulders—Charlie couldn't stop staring at his strong shoulders that begged to be released from the confines of the seams of his shirt. She felt her stomach flip-flop like she was about to talk to her crush in seventh grade.

"James!" Debra jumped off her barstool and strode over to the handsome man, her arms spread out to the sides. She reached him by the door and wrapped her arms around him in a tight hug. He leaned down to hug her back and said something to her quietly. Then he glanced up at Charlie. Charlie locked eyes with him and suddenly felt off balance.

James Maynan, the owner of Tucker Trucking.

11

Explosive Tendencies

WHY DOES HE feel familiar? Why is my mind completely obsessed with him right now? Sure, he's hot, but wow, why is my heart racing? I'm not even supposed to be near this guy, let alone talking to him.

"Jane!" Debra called as she directed James to where Charlie sat. Charlie remembered her undercover name and managed to break her gaze with James. "This is James Maynan. Tucker Trucking and Company? The place you were asking about earlier? Well, now you can ask the owner himself. James, this is Jane. She's a magazine columnist interested in our sweet little town."

A line cook walked through the half door dividing the kitchen and the counter and yelled at Debra to package up a to-go order. Debra rolled her eyes and waved her hand as if shooing a parent away that told her to leave the playground.

"I'll be right there," Debra yelled at him, slightly disappointed to be missing the fun. Turning her attention back to James and Charlie, she smiled and said, "You two hold down the fort out here, I'll be right back." Debra winked at Charlie then turned on her heel and followed the annoyed line cook to the kitchen.

James stared silently at Charlie for another moment while she pretended he wasn't making her feel like she was sitting on the sun. She glanced up at photographs on the wall and tried to focus on at least one print.

Anybody but him could have walked through that door. This isn't my fault. I can't just ignore him. Greg and Jessica will be pissed.

James appeared in her right peripherals as he leaned on the counter next to her.

"Is this seat taken?" James asked, his voice a deep, penetrating tone. He pointed to the stool next to Charlie.

Charlie didn't want to look at him but couldn't resist. She tilted her chin up towards his face and shook her head "no." James chuckled at his own joke and plopped down on the barstool in a position that felt too close to Charlie. Charlie regretted looking in his face and felt herself scoot to the left.

His blue eyes...Why didn't anybody warn me how attractive he'd be?

"I'm James," the man continued, reaching out his right hand and interrupting her thought. His eyes glittered as if a spotlight was positioned above him.

Does he realize how ridiculously attractive he is? Maybe, but not in the same way Greg does.

"Uh, hi. I'm, uh, Jane," Charlie responded with a slight apologetic smile, extending her right hand to meet his. His fingers closed around the palm of her hand, and she felt an electric motion pass between their skin. She pulled back and balled her hands into fists on her lap. She glared down at her hands as if they betrayed her.

What the hell is wrong with you, Charlie? This is the guy you're supposed to be no-contact investigating! Instead, you're drooling over him.

She couldn't help but notice the way James' pants fit his thighs perfectly or that his forearms looked like they'd be able to hold her up against a wall...

"So, you're writing about our town, huh? Sorry, was it June? Oh wait, Jane. My mistake," James said, the side of his lips tilted up in a knowing smile.

How does he know my middle name? Well, Jane and June are easy to mix up. But...he said it kind of sarcastically. He couldn't *know my middle name.*

"Yeah, Jane. Jane Blander. And correct, just writing a column about small towns and how they thrive. For instance, how Tina's place sources high quality seafood despite being landlocked. My readers will eat that sort of stuff up," Charlie said lamely then cringed.

That was a low attempt at humor, even for me.

Surprisingly James laughed out loud. The sound of his laughter was familiar, she felt like she'd heard it before. She felt like she'd been here before, in this moment. Sitting next to James, talking about nothing in particular, and he'd laughed. She was certain she knew that laugh. She felt like she was watching a rerun of Family Matters for the seventeenth time, like she had lived every moment that was unfolding.

I'm never distracted from my job, but I wish I'd met this man twenty years ago and settled down. What am I saying!?

James smiled at her, and she tried to focus back to the present, feeling confused at the blood pumping through her veins faster than normal, and the little twinge of sweat in her balled-up fists.

I'm Jane from...crap... where am I from? I can't remember...wow, he has perfect lips, like lips that I want on my neck...Charlie!

Charlie shook her head and forced herself to look James directly in the face. He was calmly talking about his business and how long it'd been around, and she had completely missed it. This topic was the whole point of her case, and she was only thinking about doing things she couldn't admit.

Maybe he'd stand up and lean over her...gently grab her hair with his hand, tilt her head back slightly...

Charlie realized James had stopped talking and was staring at her. She forced her eyes to focus. His eyebrows were arched and Charlie felt like he was searching her eyes for something, a thing Charlie couldn't touch, something she didn't know.

"So, uh, you come here often?" Charlie asked.

Original, Charlie. She felt her inner self roll its eyes.

Thankfully, Debra popped out through the half door and set down two iced teas.

"Just a few more minutes, guys, sorry. But don't you two look so cute together! Both of you curly q's! I have to admit I'm jealous of both your curls," Debra stated. She glanced at James. "Jane's work partner, Paul, he has curls, too, but they're too perfect, too put together. I think you're more Jane's style than he is, although he is dreamy."

"Now, now, Debra," James bantered back with a grin. "I know Bill is missing a few hair follicles, but you two have young kids together. Can't leave him just yet."

Debra laughed and waved her hand in the air as if she were swatting away a mosquito. Charlie couldn't help but laugh, too.

"Okay you got me. I kind of do like my husband. Jane, you get to choose between James and Paul," Debra pointed at Charlie then James laughing as she turned to return to the kitchen.

"Would you choose me, *Jane*?" James asked as he smiled at Charlie. "After all, I do own a business."

Charlie felt herself blush at his intense gaze. His eyes hadn't left hers. And he was only inches from her. She felt that if he were to touch her right now, she'd fall into his arms and never leave.

Why does he keep emphasizing that name? My real *name.*

"Depends. How do you feel about rabbits?" Charlie asked off the top of her head, trying to avoid talking about his business. She felt herself turn a whole new shade of red when she realized what she'd said.

"Well," James responded with sincerity, still not breaking their gaze, "it depends on if we're talking about the animal or the Volkswagen."

"Certainly the vehicle," Charlie said immediately, avoiding a topic she wanted to explore with the handsome stranger. But also relieved he didn't make the joke that she accidentally set him up for.

"I think their transmission is terrible, but the ride is supreme, and the experience is even better," James said.

Charlie didn't expect his enthusiasm. Nor his genuine

interest in the topic. Even better, he seemed to know the car as well as she did.

"I couldn't agree more, on all accounts," Charlie said, feeling a bit more in control as she discussed a topic she knew well. She leaned closer to James. "I have a Rabbit, it's white, and the soft top folds into the trunk. I have to admit I'm fond of it."

"Well now I have to decide if I'm going to choose you, too, right? What do I think about a girl that drives a Rabbit?" James jokingly stroked his freshly shaved chin as he observed her. Charlie felt like she was on display for a pageant show where the judges also cared about which car she drove.

"It's likely more personality than whatever junk you drive," Charlie shot back. She was beginning to enjoy the conversation. It was distracting her from his hands, and what she imagined they were capable of. Maybe if they talked a little longer, she could justify inviting him over....

You're investigating his company, Charlie! Charlie could hear Boyd yelling at her to get a grip. Instantly she was focused and knew she had to end the conversation. But she didn't want to. She wanted to step closer and lean into his chest. Feel his arms surround her.

Argh!

Once again Charlie snapped back to the conversation only to notice James staring at her. She stared back at him and a few moments passed as they searched each other eyes, neither moving. Both looking for something deep in the soul, something only the right person can find. They found it, but neither could say. Especially Charlie.

He doesn't even know who I really am. I'm not Jane! She yelled at him noiselessly. And yet, somehow, she felt he already knew that.

A door slamming shook them both from their personal daydreams and Charlie glanced at the diner's front door.

"Gr...Paul? Hi," Charlie stammered.

Who am I right now? I've never been that close to giving away Greg's identity.

James looked at Charlie with his eyebrows wrinkled then turned towards the door. Greg strode in, his chest high. He stopped at a mirror and ducked down slightly to check his hair. He ran his hands across his forehead and then turned toward James and Charlie. He froze in place.

"Jane?" Greg said towards Charlie then glared at James.

His tone told Charlie he was immediately angry, and he'd probably like to punch her.

Or get me fired.

"Hey, Paul," Charlie said with a light chuckle. "James came in while I was talking to Debra. He was giving me some information about his business and how it might align with our goals for the column."

Shouldn't have to defend myself against you, Agent Hamlin.

James glanced at Charlie with a brief confused look then nodded and glanced back at Greg. Standing up, he reached out his hand and introduced himself. Greg shook his hand but didn't give his name back.

"Jane, I have some new businesses for us to explore. I doubt we'll need Jordan's story," Greg said, his nose slightly in the air.

"It's James," James responded with a clipped tone. He picked up his iced tea and looked at Greg, his eyes squinting.

Wow, time to separate the sparring boys. More time for my daydreams another day, I suppose.

"Let's go check out that new business, then," Charlie

responded to Greg. Eyeing James she said, "Thanks for everything you told me about your company. I'm sure your input will be valuable. After all, it's not like you're just raising rabbits."

James took a sip of his tea and Charlie saw his eyes dancing in amusement. Charlie felt a rush of adrenaline falling over her and desperately wanted to feel his skin against hers.

Greg opened the door and waited for Charlie, his eyes boring into her.

Charlie stood up from the bar stool to walk towards Greg. As she passed James, she reached out and touched his forearm lightly.

"Nice to meet you, James," Charlie said.

She felt his skin raise and she wouldn't have been able to deny that hers did, too. She swore his skin was electric.

Why do I feel so sad walking away?

James watched her walk away with a concerned expression, his eyebrows furrowed.

"Be safe," James called after her.

Be safe?

Charlie forced herself to walk to the parking lot with

Greg. She could feel him seething. And Charlie knew she'd almost ruined their cover. And openly flirted with a man that was the center of her case. Failing at a case was not an option. She had to stop thinking about James.

Anyways, I can't start a relationship based on a lie. A relationship?

"What was that, Charlie? A Rabbit? Did you tell him what you drove?" Greg grabbed Charlie by the shoulder and forced her to stop after they rounded the corner of the diner's exterior wall.

"Let go of me, Greg!" Charlie said yanking away from Greg's grip. "I was making a joke about the animal, not my car. What's gotten into you?"

Greg's nostrils flared and his eyes burned into hers. He was sweating and his fists were clenched so tight his hands were turning white.

"This is supposed to be a no-contact mission, Charlie, and you're in there practically taking the man to bed," Greg replied, his lips barely moving. Every word was spit through his teeth and dripped with barely controlled rage.

"I was waiting for food when he came in, *Greg*," Charlie said with equally angry emphasis. She crossed her arms.

"Should I have hid under the barstools when he walked in?"

Charlie turned and started walking. She decided to walk back to the motel rather than hitch a ride with Greg.

"I'm not done talking to you, Charlie," Greg spit out.

Charlie kept walking. She heard Greg swear at her and say her name one more time, but she ignored him. She was furious at herself. And confused at Greg's reaction. This isn't the first time she'd broken a rule. Usually, Greg would make some joke about Boyd's paperwork and then go along with her. Not this time. He was genuinely mad.

He's frightening.

Charlie walked past the end of the building and heard voices. She glanced toward the back door of the diner and saw James and Debra talking close, both with a grim expression. James glanced over and smiled. Debra waved.

James' smile allowed her to temporarily forget Greg's odd behavior. She smiled back and waved.

"Do you need a ride somewhere, sweetie?" Debra called out.

Charlie glanced behind her and saw Greg peering out from around the corner of the building. His face was red.

Charlie could imagine horns growing out of his head. A chill pushed through her bones and settled in. She looked back at James who was watching her closely.

"Oh, I don't mind walking. Gives me a better perspective of your town," Charlie said with great effort to sound lighthearted. She smiled at the two people she wished she could get to know without a false pretense. She waved goodbye again and started walking.

Add a fake smile to a fake name and fake reason for being in your beautiful town.

Charlie felt sick. She'd never cared about being undercover. Loved making up her fake background, false name, reasons for being near someone, the whole thing. But this time, it felt different. These people didn't deserve her lies. Debra seemed to legitimately enjoy Charlie's visits to the diner. And Charlie felt comfortable around her.

And James? Well, she could feel he was just as attracted to her as she was to him. But it was more than physical attraction with James. She felt like they had a deeper connection, one that she might have felt in a dream; she longed for him. Perhaps she knew him from another life. And in that other life, they were together for a long time.

Charlie made a choice then and there to call Jessica, tell her James was innocent, then march right back to the diner to find a way to untangle her lies without letting them know she was FBI.

Nodding her head at her own decision, Charlie picked up her pace.

Charlie didn't notice Greg silently following her on foot a few buildings behind.

12

Rebellious Desire

THE NEXT DAY, Charlie didn't see Greg and the CrownVic was not in the motel parking lot. She considered knocking on his motel door and apologizing, but decided she was still mad, too. She'd talked herself out of pleading James' innocence to Jessica over the phone and instead decided to find proof.

After a quick motel breakfast, Charlie walked to the courthouse and picked up where she left off the day before. The hours passed and Charlie no longer minded that she couldn't find anything incriminating. When her stomach rumbled, Charlie realized she'd skipped lunch. She packed up her documents, turned them in, and walked back towards Tina's Place.

Debra waved at Charlie as she entered. Despite the off hour, the place was busy.

At least they're not all wearing formal gowns and running into me with boney elbows, Charlie said, amused at her own joke.

Charlie settled onto a barstool and replayed the meeting with James in her head. Glancing at the door behind her, she wished he'd walk in again.

Why am I was so attracted to him? Is it simply because Greg and my entire department told me I'm not allowed to talk to him? Or is it a real attraction?

Charlie hadn't felt attraction to anybody in her life. Sure, she'd acknowledged someone was handsome, but never felt a deep desire to be in someone's presence. And while she grew to love Tim, she never felt the desire to beg him to take her in the middle of a restaurant.

What a mix of emotions. Desire for his presence, and desire for his body. I've got to see him again. And honestly, if this case is going to go anywhere, I need to go to the warehouse. Perhaps meeting him isn't a bad thing, it gives me an in. Whether Greg approves or not!

"Hey girl, sorry it's nuts right now! Ready for some food?" Debra asked, her hair frizzed around her face.

"Yeah, sure! Just the usual, please. I'll try your recommendation next time, I promise," Charlie laughed. "Oh hey, mind giving me a ride after your shift? I want to check out that Tucker trucking place for myself."

Debra grinned.

"I'll be off by the time you've finished eating your lunch."

#

On the drive, Debra chatted about her kids and husband, allowing Charlie to silently formulate her plan in between a polite nod or mumbled mhmm. Charlie felt she was getting close to some concrete information, and she'd never been more anxious to close a case. A few minutes into the drive, Debra asked Charlie to grab her purse from behind the driver's seat.

"I forgot to tell you," Debra said pointing to her purse. "I found that picture I told you about. The one with the lady that looked like you that used to work for us."

Charlie opened Debra's orange and white flowered tote

and pulled out a faded Polaroid snap. She froze as she laid eyes on the black and white photo. Debra didn't notice and kept talking.

"I guess her name was Patricia," Debra added. "I asked the cook who has been here since God created the Earth. He said one day she just didn't show up for work and he never saw her again. That was about thirty years ago or so."

"It's impossible," Charlie whispered, staring at a photo. She felt cold, like the person staring back at her was directly from her nightmare. Except this person was beautiful, smiling.

"What is it, sweetie?" Debra asked, glancing at Charlie.

"This is my mother. But we aren't from around here. She's from Pittsburgh and I'm from Cincinnati."

"No way! How crazy is that. She's a unique looking person with those curls, just like you. Maybe this was before you were born? I can ask the cook more about her when I get back, if you want," Debra offered.

Charlie nodded, still feeling shocked.

"She looks so happy, not an expression I was used to. She is dead now, and we lost contact years ago," Charlie said.

Did my mom lie about my childhood? I wouldn't put it past her. She wasn't exactly a great mother. Could I be from around here?

Debra interrupted Charlie's thought and pointed at the gravel parking lot ahead alerting Charlie to their arrival. Charlie tried to focus on what was in front of her, but the image of her mother throwing scissors was in her vision. It felt so real. She reminded herself it was just a nightmare.

Squinting, Charlie saw a large L-shaped warehouse that was flanked by two smaller outbuildings, one with a sign "OFFICE" over the front door. Debra slowed to a stop waiting for a break in traffic, her left turn signal clicking loudly.

Click, click, click.

Every beat made Charlie tense. She was overheated now. She set the photo down afraid she'd burn a hole in it.

Run.

A black Crown Victoria turned right out of the parking lot and passed the driver's side of Debra's minivan, leaving a cloud of dust in its wake.

Click, click, click.

Sweat dripped down Charlie's back.

"Wasn't that your writing partner?" Debra looked in her side mirror with a confused expression.

"It sure looked like him," Charlie tried to say lightly, but her palms were balmy.

What the hell is Greg doing here?

Click, click, click.

"Maybe he had the same idea as me?" Charlie said, desperately trying to hide her rising fear. She felt a deep sense that something bad was about to happen.

Run!

"Debra, let's drive past and then circle back...scope it out before we pull in?"

Why was Greg at Tucker Trucking? Why did my mom lie to me?

Debra nodded, turned off her left signal, and merged back into traffic.

Debra screamed as a nearby explosion echoed through the van.

13

A Giant Tug

"PULL OFF THE road!" Charlie yelled pointing to the right. Cars honked and swerved to avoid the fireball and black smoke cloud that cascaded into the travel lanes from the direction of the warehouse.

Debra pulled the van to the side of the road and stopped, both hands squeezing the steering wheel. Charlie jumped out and glanced across the street at the warehouse and outbuildings. The fireball dissipated and the smoke found a new direction. She could see one of the outbuildings was no longer standing, heavy black smoke poured out of the rubble. Warehouse workers were running towards the building yelling and pointing.

Charlie caught her breath as she saw James exit the door of the warehouse and run towards the smoking outbuilding. She felt relief trickle through her veins and let out a burst of air.

Why do I care so much about him?

Charlie walked up to the driver's side door and Debra rolled down the window. She looked shaken and pale.

"It looks like everybody is okay, Debra. Why don't you wait here, and I'll go see if they need help. You okay to wait for me?"

"Jane, If I'd pulled in, we'd have been right next to that building. How'd you know to keep driving?" Debra asked, her face ashen. She was still gripping the steering wheel.

"I honestly don't know. But thank you for listening to me, Deb. That saved our lives," Charlie replied. She squeezed Debra's shoulder. Debra nodded shell-shocked.

Most of the traffic had cleared save for a few cars that pulled over to assist. Charlie ran across the street and through the gravel parking lot. Even undercover, an FBI agent is trained as a first responder and expected to help in an emergency. Charlie hoped there wasn't any real emergency, and she could just pop in to show her support.

"Ma'am, please stay back!" A short man approached Charlie with his palms in the air facing her.

"Hello, sir. I saw the blast as I was driving by and came to assist. Is anybody injured?" Charlie said confidently trying not to notice James commanding his troops behind the man.

"Sasha, call 9-1-1. Baron, clear the office and evacuate the warehouse. Joan, get a head count. Okay, everybody! Please move to the evacuation zone and check in with Joan. Move!" James shouted. Several people nodded and everybody moved. The workers clearly respected him.

"No, ma'am, I think we're good," the short man— Baron—replied.

Baron walked towards the warehouse and disappeared inside, following orders.

Charlie nodded and glanced at James deftly guiding his team. Standing at a distance, she still found him incredibly handsome. But this time, she felt she knew him. And not just from a silly conversation about rabbits.

Why does he look familiar? Probably a picture of him in the case file that I saw a couple weeks ago or something.

James started to walk towards the now dying fire then

stopped, noticed Charlie standing there, and rerouted to her direction.

Uhh, bad idea, Charlie! Greg is going to be pissed. Or rather, more pissed.

"Hey," James said. His eyes were squinting against the sunlight, but he smiled at Charlie, showing all his teeth.

"Hey," Charlie said, mesmerized.

"What brought you around these parts?" James asked, stepping a little closer.

"Oh, I was driving by, with Debra," Charlie pointed to the minivan, "and heard the blast. I stopped to see if anybody was hurt."

"Ah, well, I don't believe so. The building that blew was our records department. Our records employee doesn't work on Thursdays, thankfully." James seemed to be studying her face, her hair.

"I'm happy to hear that..." Charlie trailed off

James tilted his head slightly to the right. Charlie reminded herself to breathe. Neither heard any noises around them. The firetruck pulling through the gravel driveway with the sirens blaring was soundless. James' blue eyes only saw Charlie, and Charlie coveted his wavy hair, his strong shoulders, and how attracted she felt to him.

"James, sorry to interrupt," Baron said walking towards James.

James and Charlie startled, as if another explosion had occurred.

"Buildings are clear and everybody is accounted for. The Sheriff and Fire Captain are enroute," Baron said.

The sirens of a firetruck sliced through the air, the gravel crunched underneath large tires.

James broke eye contact, the moment ended. With a quick farewell nod, James walked over to meet the firemen.

"Sorry, ma'am. Were you here when the explosion happened? Are you okay?" Baron asked, his kind eyes worried. He was much older, slightly hunched over, thinned grey hair gathered in a ponytail near his neck.

Charlie watched James walk away, annoyed at the man for interrupting the surreal experience.

What was that, anyways?

"No, I was driving by. Stopped to help but seems you got it all under control. I'm sorry you lost your records building," Charlie offered. Her knees felt weak.

Probably just an adrenaline crash, Charlie mused. But she knew that something had passed between her and James. Something genuine. A connection.

I miss him.

"James will figure it out," Baron said, oblivious to Charlie's state of mind. "He's keen, like his dad. I'm sure we have some redundancy for the important stuff. Funny thing, speaking of James' dad, you look so much like the family that started this business...the likeness is uncanny! Those curls!" Baron laughed.

"Who started this business?" Charlie asked, tugging on a curl near her shoulders.

James called for Baron and waved him over.

"Take care, ma'am," Baron said. He dipped his head and walked towards James and the swarm of fireman.

Charlie turned to leave, then glanced back over her shoulder at the group. James was staring at her with a curious gaze. He gave her a little wave then faced the men. She regarded him for a moment. Taking a deep breath, she looked away and walked back to Debra.

I look like James' family?

#

Greg was leaning against the wall by the front door of the diner when Charlie and Debra returned. Charlie could tell he was still angry. Charlie felt a little bit of fear settle in her gut.

Still running off adrenaline, Debra started to blurt out witnessing the explosion when Charlie interrupted her.

"Debra was taking me to a restaurant in Old Mill, and we passed Tucker Trucking as an explosion happened," Charlie lied. She looked at Debra and shrugged. Debra nodded, following Charlie's lead.

"Thanks again for taking me on a girl's day, Debra. Sorry our last outing didn't work out," Charlie said with a frown.

"Be careful," Debra whispered, hugging Charlie. She nodded goodbye to Greg and walked off. Greg watched through narrowed eyes until she was out of sight.

"I told you to stay away from there and you drive right by it!" Greg shouted at Charlie furiously. He pointed at Charlie's face. "You could have been killed!"

"Greg what has gotten in to you lately?" Charlie said. She held her position. "You're acting like you're in charge of me. We're partners, we're supposed to plan and act together! I just wanted different food! And besides, what "random tip" did you receive earlier that was so important you storm out? You keep your secrets, and I keep mine!" Charlie said crossing her arms. Despite an unsettled feeling surrounding her muscles, she was also sick of Greg's childish behavior.

Greg sighed and rocked back onto his heels. He relaxed his fists and took a deep breath.

"I was told there might have been a connection to another trucking company up north," Greg said, resigned.

"And you couldn't share that simple information with me?" Charlie glared at him.

He may be calming down, but I'm just getting started!

"I'm sorry. You're right," Greg took in another deep breath and exhaled. "Is there any paperwork we need to do regarding the explosion? Was anybody hurt? Did you assist?"

Only that I disappeared into my wannabe boyfriend's aura for a few moments and was rudely interrupted by a short, but kind, man.

"No, nobody was hurt, nor did I assist. I stopped, I

checked in with the foreman, and left," Charlie said. "I did what any other passerby would have done."

"Alright. And you're sure you're not hurt?"

"Greg, I'm fine. Now what connection did you find with the other company?"

Greg looked off to the side.

"Okay, that was a lie," Greg admitted. "I heard from another agent at the Albany field office that the owner of Tucker Trucking, James Maynan, may also be guilty of a few unsolved murders in town."

"What?" Charlie felt as if somebody punched her in the stomach.

Hold it together, Charlie!

"I don't believe it," Charlie added as she pulled her shoulders back.

"Well, you should. I'm not supposed to tell you that because we're only on surveillance. So I went to check out some of those cases at a courthouse up north. That was the tip. I didn't find anything solid, but a few possible links. It's likely validated."

"Greg!" Charlie crossed her arms. "That's a big deal! You should have told me sooner."

The man I met certainly didn't seem capable of murder, Charlie thought, recalling his gaze on her.

"Charlie, please, I'm telling you now, okay?" Greg reached out and squeezed her shoulder. His version of a comforting touch, but Charlie pulled away. His touch felt vile, like he was initiating a curse.

"You're strong and capable, but you're not 100% back on your feet yet. I'll share the information I found, and you can help me on the data side. Stay away from James for a while until we know. I don't like the interest he's taken in you. And now clearly someone is out to get him. I don't want you tangled up in that. Please let me protect you at least a little bit?" Greg's eyes pleaded with her to agree.

She didn't agree. And she knew deep in her gut that he was still lying to her.

I know you were there, too, Greg, Charlie's mind screamed.

I don't trust you; I never have.

...and it's time I find out why.

Time to play your game.

"It's nice to have someone look out for me. I'm sorry, I'm not used to that. You're absolutely right. I'd love to look at the information you've collected and see what I can find out," Charlie said with a polite smile.

I'm a trained undercover agent. I can play you like a fiddle.

Greg stared at her for a moment, then coming to his own conclusions, smiled back. The hair on Charlie's neck stood up and she shivered.

"I'm sorry I stormed out earlier."

"I forgive you."

"Want to actually eat now?" Greg asked gesturing to the diner door.

"May as well, my plans were a bit deterred," Charlie said with a fake laugh. Greg opened the door and allowed her to go first.

"So what exactly happened, anyways, at the warehouse? What all did you see?" Greg asked as he led them to their corner booth.

Charlie slid in, forgetting the raised metal seam on the corner of the table. Her sweater grabbed the sharp edge and the wool frayed.

"Oh no! The table caught my sweater," Charlie frowned. "Darn it, I didn't bring enough clothes as it is."

"You can fix it, can't you? I've seen your master sewing skills," Greg said with a rigid smile.

Charlie recalled a stakeout they'd been on together when Greg had jokingly flexed his arms at her and popped a seam in the sleeve. He'd been embarrassed and proud at the same time. She'd taken his shirt and fixed the seam in less than a minute with a sewing kit she kept in her purse. Greg hadn't put the shirt back on for an hour because he said he wanted to admire her work. He'd ended up pursuing a bad guy shirtless that night. A moment in their relationship where she'd thought maybe her intuition was wrong.

"I didn't bring my sewing stuff," Charlie chuckled. She tied a knot on the frayed edge and figured she'd find a sewing kit at a gas station tomorrow.

A waitress came by and took their orders. Charlie made up a brief story of her so-called "girl's day" with Debra and how they were supposed to end the day with food and cocktails when the explosion happened. The odds of passing the warehouse were high, considering there are only three main roads in between the two towns. Debra was shaken up, so they decided it was best to head home and go out another day.

"I'm glad you weren't hurt," Greg said. He reached out towards Charlie, as if to touch her, then thought better and put his hand back on his lap.

"I do feel a bit of a headache from the blast, though," Charlie admitted after they'd finished eating.

"Alright," Greg said. "How about you go rest in the motel for an hour, and I'll go make copies of the cases I received earlier. I will meet you in one hour and we can go over my notes. And yes, I made clear and concise notes for you. Sure you're feeling well enough to walk back?"

"I'm fine. It will be good to rest for a little bit, though," Charlie admitted as she got up from the diner booth, careful to avoid the sharp edge this time. Her ribs were healing well, but sudden movements—like a blast— reminded her she wasn't one hundred percent yet.

Greg waved as he pulled away in the Crown Vic, heading west. Charlie watched him disappear at the first left turn and took a deep breath.

Like a fiddle...

14

Ripped Sweaters and Briefcase Secrets

CHARLIE WENT BACK inside the diner and asked the unfamiliar waitress to use the telephone. She was given permission and dialed Jessica. Jessica answered on the first ring.

"Jess, things are getting weird here. Apparently, my mom used to work at a local diner, and a random worker at Tucker Trucking says I look like James Maynan's family. And Jess, he keeps calling me June!" Charlie said. Charlie told Jessica about the explosion, the photograph, and the conversations with James, hinting at her attraction.

"Sheesh, Charlie. What have we gotten you involved in? This was promised to be an easy case!" Jessica said after

Charlie finished. Then Jessica paused. "Is he hot?"

"Jessica! Well yes, but...there's more..." Charlie took a deep breath. "Something is up with Greg."

"Like what?" Jessica asked carefully.

"He's been overprotective, lying about trivial things, and...I saw him leave Tucker Trucking right before the explosion. He stormed out at lunch and said he was going to check on a lead. When I came back, I told him I was going to lunch with someone and just happened to be passing. He was so angry but played it off like he was trying to protect me and my poor injured self," Charlie rolled her eyes. "The only thing that calmed him down was me pretending like I enjoyed him being worried about me...Jess? You still there?"

"Yeah, sorry. Yeah, I'm still here," Jessica said. She was quiet for another moment. "Charlie, I wasn't ready to tell you this, because it's probably nothing." She paused again.

"Uh-oh. Hit me with it," Charlie said wondering what Jessica could possibly have to add.

"Years ago, a tip came in from an unknown source that Greg blackmailed his way into the FBI role. Remember my reaction in Buffalo? I knew I had heard his name but figured no way it could be true once I met him. The agent that received the tip didn't feel it was credible, either, likely related to a previous case or someone harboring a grudge, so no action was taken. But after what happened with Hen, I figured it'd be a good idea to follow up."

"Are you kidding me? What did you find out?" Charlie asked incredulous.

It could be true.

"I originally heard of this before Greg was even part of our team, so I tabled it. Then recently...I don't know. I decided to follow up on it. I managed to track the source to New York City and went up there when you were in the hospital two months ago. To be safe, I sent Greg on an assignment a few states away to verify he couldn't harm you in the hospital...you know...just in case. I don't take chances. Boyd didn't know. Again, this tip was old. I didn't believe it could be true, either. Unfortunately, I had no luck, the trail went cold. Up until now, we haven't had any concrete reason to doubt Greg."

"Until now," Charlie repeated. "What do you want me to do? He has the car right now."

"I was going to ask why you didn't take the car I

assigned you."

"Huh? Greg told me there was a shortage and we only had one car, like what happened when we drove to Buffalo."

"That's not true, Charlie. I assigned you both one, as usual. I left the two sets of keys on my desk. Although, I was gone all day, so something could have changed with the fleet, I guess. Why would he force you into one car?"

"I don't know, but I'm certainly going to find out."

"Just watch your back, Char. Keep your eye on him, but try to act normal as if nothing had changed. I'll keep digging. Oh. One more thing. Robbie, your mechanic, called me. He said to have you call him when you can about your Volkswagen."

Charlie promised to call Robbie and keep a watchful eye on Greg. They agreed to check in with each other the next afternoon. She hung up and felt relief that she didn't have to argue with her intuition anymore. She'd always known Greg was bad news, but like Jessica said, there had been no reason to believe it. He'd always been respectful, well-admired, awarded, and above the line.

Maybe James is innocent and this whole thing is a fraud

assignment, Charlie wished. *Yeah, that makes sense.*

Charlie rolled her eyes at herself as she walked out of Tina's Cafe. Her partner was possibly a bad agent, and she was worried about some man in her case being innocent.

James doesn't feel like some *man in any case. But he thinks I'm just a magazine columnist; he'd never want me in his life once he finds out that I've been investigating him and lying about everything...except the Rabbit, of course.*

Charlie turned east towards the motel and admired the brick-faced shops of downtown Mulrose. The air was humid as Charlie strolled across the parking lot and crossed the street. She noticed dark clouds on the horizon and made a note to carry her raincoat if she went out later. Walking at a leisurely pace, she peered into display windows, but her mind was rehashing her conversation with Jessica and trying to process how everything had suddenly changed.

No wonder Jessica waited to tell me about Greg; I'd have cut ties with him a long time ago. What is Greg up to? If it's true, why would he need to forge his way into the FBI? And who called in the tip?

The buildings showed signed of aging, but the

storefronts were polished and modern. As Charlie was about to round the corner to Admiral, she saw a blinking red sign in a dirty window advertising a seamstress. Unlike the others, this storefront had an air of abandonment hovering in the eaves. She paused in front of the splintered wooden door and ran her fingers over the knotted fibers in her favorite teal sweater. She decided to stop to see if the seamstress was in and could repair the threads before the whole thing unraveled. The delay would give her time to think and plan before running into Greg. Plus, she was beginning to sweat from the oppressive humidity.

Charlie pushed open the heavy wooden door and walked through the doorway.

A metal holiday bell jingled against the wood as the door slammed shut behind her.

She felt herself go cold; the images of her nightmare surfaced. She stopped in the entrance, the jangle bouncing around her ears. She felt herself being pulled into a daydream.

"Hello?" A female voice said from the back of the room.

Charlie shook her head to stop the nightmare from fully

forming in her head.

"I'm looking for a small wool sweater repair," she responded to the voice. "Or even just the tools to do it myself."

A dim overhead light illuminated a well-worn path through the carpet to the counter and the back workroom. Charlie looked around at the disheveled shelves, filled to the brim with sewing machine parts, fabrics, tools and accessories. Glancing up, Charlie was startled by a small-framed elderly lady with thin gray hair falling over her pale, weathered face, behind the counter like she'd been standing there the whole time.

"You okay?" The old lady chuckled. "I don't believe we have any ghosts here so maybe you're gawking at this mess." She laughed again, a raspy breathless tone. She gestured towards the dusty shelves. "The last person that owned this place kept everything organized, down to the last pin. But that was thirty years ago... things have changed." Shaking her head, the lady walked around the counter and approached Charlie. "Sorry, what can I do for you?"

Charlie breathed in as deeply as she could to settle her

heartbeat. Her ribs pulsed. The whole room felt like it was closing in. Her heartbeat pounded in her ears. The feeling of premonition swelled in her gut.

Run. Stay. Be ready.

Forcing a smile, and holding the edge of her sweater up, Charlie ignored the voices and said, "I snagged my..."

"Ooh wow. Oh wow!" The lady interrupted loudly. Stepping in closer, she eyed Charlie. Charlie stepped back, confounded and uncomfortable.

"Thirty years!" The old lady suddenly appeared to have lost fifty-years of age in her excitement. She threw her hands in the air and spun in a circle, her thin hair a spiraled nest. "She was right! Thirty-years later! Those damn curls. 'Just look for the curls', she'd said. Oh, this is so exciting. She said you'd find your way back here!" She stepped in close to Charlie again and reached out with spiny fingers. Grabbing Charlie's left hand, and looking into her eyes, she patted Charlie's hand. "Wait, wait right here."

Charlie wobbled back unevenly as the lady released her hand and skittered through the mess to the backroom. She could feel her heartbeat frantically echoing throughout her chest.

What in the world is going on?!

Charlie desperately wanted to leave, but she was curious. She turned around and looked at the holiday bell on the wooden door. The bell from her nightmares.

Why is it so familiar? Why does it frighten me?

Suddenly, Charlie remembered. Her mouth dropped open as a flood of memories consumed her like fire on a match.

> *Mother was wearing an apron, no, a half-sewn shirt. I was about three and investigating the shelves as a toddler does. Mother had told me over and over again to stay in the workroom. But I forgot... and found myself by the front door with a box of fabric pins. I was trying to make a pyramid. Mom yelled for me to get back in the backroom and threw something at me. It was a pair of scissors. The scissors landed sharp point down in my arm. I screamed and fell onto the pyramid of pins, my head hitting the door. The holiday bell jingled above my head.*

The nightmares, they came from a memory this place! A tailor shop!

She looked at her left arm and the scar that remained.

Everything Mother told me about my young childhood was fake. She told me this scar was from a jungle gym.

Charlie heard rummaging and various noises from the backroom and the old lady mumbling to herself. A final "aha!" and the old lady half-walked, half-jogged back across the worn carpet carrying a tattered, black leather briefcase with both hands. Charlie turned toward her, but still felt deep in her nightmare, just a different version.

"Patricia wanted you to have this when the time came," the old lady said. She reached her hands out, offering the briefcase to Charlie. "The handle broke many years ago, but I don't think you'll mind so much once you see what is inside."

"My...Mother left this?" Charlie asked, choking a little bit.

Charlie pictured the flowers she'd picked from her garden the night she received the message from the lawyer about her mother's death.

"Yes, darling. She carried a lot of regret. She didn't spend a dime of the settlement and made sure you could go anywhere you wanted to when she passed away. Patricia wanted to tell you the truth but never knew how. When she found out she was sick, she left me this briefcase."

"The settlement? This seamstress shop, it was hers. I remember it now. Who are you?" Charlie asked, trying to piece together what she was hearing.

Charlie had never called the lawyer back despite his multiple attempts to contact her. She hadn't wanted anything that belonged to her mother.

Charlie retrieved the briefcase from the lady's spiny fingers and glanced around. She knew why the carpet was stained red to her right. It was about ten in the morning, and she'd spilled her Kool-Aid. She'd been sent the corner for the rest of the day with no food.

A tear surfaced and slid down Charlie's cheek.

The left side of the counter had Charlie's name scratched into it.

I don't think Mother ever discovered that. Otherwise, I might have been dead.

"I'm nobody important, dear," the lady replied kindly. She reached up and brushed Charlie's chin with soft flick. Patting the briefcase in Charlie's tight grasp, she said kindly, "I hope you find the answers you need."

15

Motel Tussle

CHARLIE WALKED TOWARD her motel without seeing anything. Her mind was looking around the petite town through the eyes of a four-year-old. A past Charlie somehow now remembered so clearly. The cafe, the tailor shop, the train station, the streets. Every spot had some reminder of how abusive Mother had become. Memories flooded back; painful memories of neglect and abuse. They'd left this town abruptly when she was five. Somewhere in her adolescent years she'd conveniently forgotten this town. Her life didn't get any better after the sudden move. She and her mother moved into a single wide trailer at Envert Trailer Park in a forgotten town north of Cincinnati. Her mother managed to continue making money as a tailor. Sometimes Charlie would feel she respected Mother's drive, always making money despite her circumstances. Mother would find new clients by hanging out near the upscale stores with her sewing portfolio ready to show off. Didn't hurt that she was beautiful. Mother's cheekbones were defined, her waistline smaller than her hips, her weight a respectful size 6 or 8 depending on what type of alcohol she'd chosen that month. Those alcoholic nights are what told Charlie she needed to leave her mother to survive...

> *Mother attended fancy parties while I hitched rides to school and fought off trailer park creeps. I knew how to cook a full meal by age five, as Mother would expect food when she returned from work. I had to wait until seven to start school and had to find my own transportation, because the trailer park didn't have a bus route. Sometimes I'd catch a ride from the farmer that lived on the land behind our trailer, but even getting to his fence line was about a mile. Other times I'd walk, and*

boy were those winters harsh. Every day I'd leave school early to be home in time to prepare dinner for Mother. She'd slap me on the hands or across the face if I didn't have food to cook. Or send me out to find something. Mother seemed to make good money, and at that age, I never understood how it disappeared.

The only benefit for me of Mother's job, is she'd often have extra fabrics from client projects and I learned to make my own clothes from that. If one seam wasn't up to standards, Mother would cut up the entire garment and tell me to start over or go without. Despite our living situation, Mother required me to always be clean, dressed in perfectly tailored clothes, as Mother could never let her clients know how she truly lived. Fortunately I learned fast and became a talented seamstress. I always appeared in school as well-clothed and high-end. No way would I ever let anybody know I came from the Envert Trailer Park.

One evening when I was eight, I asked Mother about my dad and what happened to him. In response, Mother flipped the table over, flinging the squash salad I'd just made on the wall. 'Don't ever ask about your bitch of a father and his family again!' She'd yelled then went to her bedroom slamming the door, leaving me ducked in the corner of the living room crying. I don't remember if I cried because I was disappointed at not knowing what happened to my dad, or the waste of the dinner that I'd had to steal to get. I hated stealing.

That was the last time I'd cried, though. I made it to fifteen in that house just ducking my head and existing only in my daydreams. I sewed a lot. By then, Mother had some lung illness that she refused to treat. I left Mother's *one night after yet another violent outburst. After six months living in an alley behind a retail store I worked at, I saved enough money to rent a dingy one-room flat above the Gator General Store.*

The desk attendant flagged Charlie down as she crossed the motel lobby hugging the briefcase. Charlie stopped mid-stride and tried to focus on the shy attendant. Her memories of Envert Trailer Park remained on the surface. She felt defeated, confused...alone.

She wished she could share this remembered past with Debra. Or fall into James' arms and cry. She rarely felt lonely. Being alone was safe; she never disappointed or hurt herself.

I'm fine. I'll get over this stuff. It doesn't change my life or anything. If that were true, though, why does it hurt so much?

"Two messages for you, Miss. First, Paul says he'll be late to your meeting. Second, a Jessica called and asked that you return her call immediately," the attendant said, handing her two strips of paper with scrawled pen work.

Charlie wondered what Greg was up to, and why he had

to leave a message at the motel he was supposedly staying at himself. Nonetheless, Charlie nodded politely as she retrieved the papers from the attendant's outstretched hand.

I wonder if Jessica found something!

"Thank you. How long ago did Paul leave this message?" Charlie lifted up the message with Paul's name on it.

"About an hour ago, I believe, Miss," the attendant said confidently. He eyed Charlie's curls and traced her body lines down to her feet.

"Got it, I will return the calls from my room," Charlie said, annoyed at the forwardness of the young attendant.

He smiled at Charlie and watched her walk to the interior lobby door. Charlie shivered despite the building afternoon heat and walked up the stairs towards her room. Still lost in memories and recollections of her childhood, she wondered what Mother left in this briefcase and wondered how to prepare herself for what she may find.

Charlie set the briefcase gently on her bed then stepped back and stared at the worn case with animosity. She turned on the air conditioning unit to relieve the room of the oppressive heat and decided to try Jessica before opening the suitcase. She kept the briefcase in eyesight as she dialed Jessica. After several rings, neither Jessica nor her assistant answered, and the answering machine did not pick up.

Jessica is terrible at deleting voice messages, the tape is probably full.

Charlie set the phone in the cradle and went back to considering the briefcase. She grabbed a pink button up linen shirt and carefully set her torn wool sweater aside, temporarily forgetting about the pull in the threads.

Am I ready for this? Charlie wondered as she observed the aging of the leather.

"Mother, what did you do now?" Charlie said to nobody. She didn't know whether to feel apprehensive, scared, excited, or even annoyed.

She took a deep breath and reached for the press locks on the top of the briefcase as the air conditioning unit moaned in the background.

A knock on the door startled her and she froze.

"Charlie? It's me," Greg's voice boomed through the door. "Sorry I'm late. Can I come in?"

Charlie glanced at the door behind her then back at the briefcase. She shoved the briefcase under the pillows at the head of the bed and straightened the comforter.

"I'm coming!" Charlie crossed the room and opened the door just enough to make it obvious to Greg she didn't want him entering.

Greg stared at her for a moment then leaned over to look at the bed behind her, appearing to search for something.

Charlie pretended not to notice, but her hand tightened on the interior door handle.

"Hey Greg, any luck on those leads?"

In response, Greg's face went from tan to sunburnt then back to tan in a flash. Charlie thought maybe she made it up. But something was irking Greg.

He seems to be unraveling, Charlie observed. *But which thread did I tug?*

"Did you rest?" Greg asked under his breath. He seemed to be struggling to stay in control of his patience.

Charlie tried to shrug, intentionally keeping her body language neutral.

"I haven't had an opportunity yet. I was just settling in

when you knocked. Think we could chat over dinner? We talked about trying a different place tonight. Or maybe go back to the first place and actually get a table?" Charlie offered. She thought a joke would help, but the air hung heavy with tension.

This time she didn't bother to smile. Neither did Greg.

They stared at each other, as if assessing an adversary.

He knows I know about him now, but how? Charlie wondered. She stood up straighter; felt on-guard. *But what do I even know?*

"What time should I be ready?" Charlie asked, desperately trying to lighten her tone. She wasn't prepared for a stand-off right now. He'd caught her vulnerable, like skin from a freshly ripped Band-Aid.

I don't even slightly understand what is going on here!

"How about four-thirty," Greg replied coldly.

Charlie nodded and closed the door while Greg stood there staring her down.

Charlie leaned against the closed door for a moment listening to Greg's steps. His room was only two doors away, but he seemed to walk more steps than necessary to reach his door. Eventually his footsteps faded. Charlie didn't hear an elevator or stairwell door open.

Where is he going?

Charlie gave up listening and walked away from the door. She decided to try to call Jessica again. Unfortunately, there was still no answer from either woman nor the answering machine.

Charlie started to feel concerned about the lack of contact. And at the very least, the answering machine would say, "You've reached Special Agent Jessica Chance...".

What did Jessica need when she called the motel? Jessica can take care of herself, but what if she found out more about Greg? I hope she's okay.

Pulling the briefcase out from under the pillows, Charlie remembered Jessica told her to check in with the mechanic about the Rabbit. Once again eyeing the briefcase, she dialed Robbie. She looked forward to hearing more about her car, a conversation about something she understood.

I could really use an aggressive drive in my car right about now.

Robbie answered on the second ring.

"Hey Charlie, been trying to get a hold of you for a few days. I did find something unusual in the Rabbit," Robbie said.

"Sorry, Robbie. Small towns don't offer a lot of contact opportunities when you're undercover," Charlie replied.

"I'd rather you see it in person," Robbie hesitated," but I know you said you're out of town...I found a GPS unit under the rear axle. Now I'm no agent, but I assume you don't tag your personal vehicles."

"No, we don't," Charlie responded quietly. She felt her stomach tightening. "There is no reason that should be there. Did you find an antenna, too?" Charlie sat down on the edge of the bed and put her right hand on the briefcase as she waited for Robbie to respond.

What other surprises should I prepare for today?

"Yeah, right up through the trunk liner."

"How long does it look like it's been there?"

"It's not too dirty or worn, so maybe a couple months?"

"Is it still transmitting?"

"Yeah, I checked with my radio. I didn't disconnect it, wanted you to know first."

"Thanks, Robbie. Would you mind putting her in the

basement of that parking garage on Cherry Hill? That should block the transmission for now. I will check it out when I return. I have a feeling we're nearly done with this case."

Robbie agreed and disconnected.

Greg probably bugged my car in the event I refused to share a ride with him on this case.

Fueled by irritation, Charlie slammed the phone down and considered approaching Greg and demanding answers. She raised her right fist to punch the bed but remembered the briefcase. Taking a deep breath, she popped open the briefcase.

Maybe I'll find what I need here. If not, I'm over this cat and mouse crap.

Housed in the dusty liner of the aged briefcase was a mixture of black and white photographs, newspaper clippings, an ink pen with the monogram "TT", a full, sealed envelope with "Charlie" scrawled across the middle in blue ink, an old sewing kit Charlie recognized as Mother's purse kit, a crude pencil drawing of what appeared to be a family tree, and a manila folder thick with documents. The manila folder showed a stamp in the upper left corner that said "Colmstock & Jones".

The lawyer found a way to get me the documents from Mother's estate despite my resistance to return his many calls.

Shoving the folder away, Charlie timidly picked up a photograph with frayed corners and caught her breath. She recognized her mother, probably in her late teens, wrapped in the arms of some man. Mother was smiling. *Boy was she beautiful*, Charlie thought. Charlie had never seen a photo of her dad before, but she knew immediately the man in the photo was her father. The man had a head full of tight curls and stern lips. It was like looking at a photo of herself.

They both look so happy...what happened to him?

She felt her eyes dampen. Picking up another photo, Charlie recognized one of the outbuildings at Tucker Trucking... the one with "OFFICE" written over the door. In front stood the same smiling man and woman. Her father held a bottle of champagne, and Mother two flute glasses. Off to the side of the photograph stood a much younger, but recognizable, Baron, the foreman of Tucker Trucking. On the back of the photograph, "Hank and Patricia, 1958," was written in fancy cursive.

"You look so much like the family that started this business...the likeness is uncanny," Charlie remembered Baron saying the day of the explosion.

"It wasn't James Maynan he referred to as 'the family', but my own parents," Charlie said out loud in sudden bewilderment. "My family started Tucker Trucking?"

I don't know how much more information I can process. Maybe I shouldn't look through this stuff. I am doing just fine without rehashing my childhood.

But I want to know the truth about my dad, and why Mother took me away from him suddenly.

Feeling overwhelmed but determined, Charlie picked up the next item: a newspaper clipping from August 3, 1942. The heading read,

"Old Mill Celebrates Tucker and June Winslow, Owners of Tucker Trucking & Freight"

A black and white photograph below the header showed a dainty, curly-haired woman standing sternly next to an unsmiling tall, dark-haired man. The woman was holding an infant wrapped tightly in a printed blanket. The small caption under the image read, "Mr. Winslow cut the ribbon on Tucker Trucking & Freight after nine months of construction. His wife, June Winslow, and infant son, Hank, joined the celebration."

Charlie never knew she received her middle name from her grandmother. She stared at the image and took in her grandparents. It was obvious the curly hair had been passed down for generations. She studied the solemn expressions of the adults. They appeared focused, in the moment. The infant child, who would become her father, was lost in the black and white pixels with no discernible traits, a blanket around his face.

Charlie bristled as the air conditioning unit shut off suddenly with a groan. She reached for the next article with a sigh when she heard soft scraping sounds coming from the doorknob of her room. She set the article back down and quietly lowered the lid of the briefcase while the lock-picking sounds continued. Charlie glanced at the safe by the door where her gun was stored. She knew she couldn't open it without alerting the intruder, as the buttons beeped when entering the code. Charlie made a quick decision and tiptoed to the corner of the room by the telephone, out of view from the doorway as the intruder continued working on the lock.

With a final click, the door opened, and cautious footsteps entered the room.

Charlie tried to steady her breathing and listen over the sound of her rapidly rising heart rate and racing thoughts.

The footsteps briefly hesitated at the door, then seemingly comfortable with the silence, feet approached the bed. Charlie pressed herself against the wall as a tall, hooded figure with a black face mask, baggy black pants, and black combat boots came into view. Charlie kept herself calm as she observed the black figure lift the lid of the briefcase and reach for the first photo, the photo of her parents celebrating with champagne.

Charlie walked two soundless steps from the wall towards the bed and jumped on the intruder's back, wrapping her arm around his neck.

"That's mine!" Charlie yelled. She felt herself flush with all the emotion she'd been repressing and squeezed as hard as she could. "I've had enough!"

Gloved hands reached up and hooked under her arms. With one tug, he released her arms from around his neck and tossed her off. Charlie yelped as she fell to the floor but jumped up as the assailant whipped around. She caught him with a punch from her right fist, and he stumbled back slightly. Lunging at him again, the assailant blocked her punch and shoved her backwards. She landed hard against the wall, her ribs immediately crying out for her to stop. Instead of listening, she stepped forward. She again made contact between his cheek and her fist. The intruder recoiled but reached out and grabbed both her wrists. Charlie grunted as he spun her around and slammed her back against his chest; Charlie's arms crossed in front of her, and he tightened his arms around her. She wiggled and kicked and tried to bite.

A gloved hand deftly put a cloth over her nose and mouth, his arm around her a steel rope.

Charlie tried to hold her breath but within moments, she fell limp into the intruder's arms.

16

Rolling in the Hay

THE FLASHLIGHT PIERCED through Charlie's eyelids again.

"Stop," she begged to whomever was out there, her voice hoarse. She was not fully awake. Her eyes felt swollen, ragged, like they had for many days following Tim's death. She'd cried for three days straight and only stopped because her eyelids completely swelled shut.

Tim, I miss you every day, she thought, her mind lost somewhere outside of consciousness. She missed the simplicity of those days. The routine. She wished she'd enjoyed it more.

The light passed across her face. Charlie knew she was lying on the ground; her slender frame curled around itself. She couldn't understand why she was sleeping on the ground. She was overheated and sweaty. Perhaps she was dreaming; a lover's arms, wrapped around her, probably lounging in bed at first, but having rolled off in a tangled heat, she must have stayed on the ground.

But this reality felt different. Less cozy. Charlie was stiff, confused, like she'd forgotten to move for three days. Her skin was itchy. She could only grasp reality in clipped moments, then she'd slip back into darkness.

The flashlight passed her eyes again.

So bright. Mother?

"Enough!" Charlie said with a ragged breath. She peered through her swollen eyelids to see who was around, her breaths short. Nobody. No flashlight. The humidity was stifling.

Where am I? Why is the air conditioning off?

The light flashed again. She squinted against the brightness, everything in her vision illuminated to a pure white.

Lightning, she realized.

Charlie squeezed her eyes closed, releasing little droplets of tears. Trying again, she squinted into the room;

her eyelids barely tolerating the movement. Before her sprawled a dusty, rectangular room. The ceiling, walls, and floors were all covered in large panel wood, dark with age and use. Three stalls loomed behind her, the smell of must clung to every surface. Cloudy daylight shone through a lone window at the peak of the a-frame, lightning illuminating the dust like confetti in the air every time it sparked.

A barn?

The other side of the room lay in shadows, its features unclear.

Rolling over on her side, she stiffened when she realized the scratchy material of her makeshift bed was hay.

Nononono, anything but hay! Where's my purse? I don't have my EpiPen!

She sat up quickly, intending to move away from the hay pile. Closing her eyes again she struggled to fight off the rush of blackness that flashed across her vision. She tried to catch her breath, but it seemed her heart was racing too fast to normalize her breathing. She clenched her jaw, as the memory of her last experience with hay washed over her and tried to take control. She looked down at her legs and sipped air.

Lightning flashed and thunder immediately echoed off the empty walls, the lightning reflecting off something shiny by her foot. She reached out and found a silver cuff clamped around her left ankle attached to a rusty chain. The chain ran across the floor and disappeared into the darkness of the middle stall about five feet from where she sat.

Fifteen years with the Bureau, and I've been tied up twice just this year, she surmised.

Despite her intensifying struggle to breathe, she felt momentarily annoyed rather than panicked. She'd been in dangerous situations, sure. Life threatening? Absolutely. But these two cases...

It is all wrong. Everything has gone wrong. And now I'm tied up in hay, Charlie thought. *It had to be hay.*

The hay...maybe she was a little scared. Her annoyance shifted back to fear.

Charlie felt a new wave of panic wash over her as her breathing tightened and reality hit her in the gut.

What happened to Greg?

The last thing she remembered was ripping her sweater

on the table at Tina's diner.

"Greg!" Charlie yelled looking around again, this time fully awake.

Okay, there's the door, she thought, spotting an aged barn door off to her left. *That's a start.*

She started yanking on the ankle cuff, trying to free her foot.

Focus, you're trained for this, Charlie. This is nothing new. You're just working.

She remembered looking for a seamstress downtown.

"Greg! Where are you?!" Charlie yelled again, her breath coming in short, raspy clips.

No, no that's not all.

The call with Jessica...the briefcase...the fight in the hotel room. She remembered the cloth over her face.

I'll kill Greg if he did this.

Charlie's throat felt like a thousand fire ants had eaten their way down her esophagus, her nightmare reflecting images through her conscious. Her body ached. She grasped the silver cuff around her ankle with all her strength and attempted to squeeze her foot through, her ankle bone bruising from the effort. She looked up at the window as the lightning flashed immediately followed by bone vibrating thunder.

I must get out of here! If the hay doesn't kill me the weather will!

Charlie pulled herself onto her hands and knees and started crawling closer to the termination of the chain. The hay swirled in fine, deadly refractions throughout the air, tickling her face. The scraping of the metal chain across the floor mixed with the thunder clambering outside. The rain began to fall; a panicked pitch clawing at the tin roof. Charlie was panting now, her elbows felt weak, her back begging to sag into the wooden, hay-strewn floor.

Charlie felt herself losing consciousness.

Lowering herself to the floor, her most feared memory coursing through her like an earthquake, she collapsed into the fearful, crushing blackness...

Charlie and her best friend – what is his name? – are taking shelter in her neighbor's barn during an unexpected thunderstorm. Mother has warned her about going in there, but her best friend says it is safer than running home with all the lightning streaking through the sky.

She's six and he's nine. She trusts him because he looks out for her when nobody else does. Although storms don't bother them, they know that even a small thunderstorm can turn fierce in an instant around here. The wind starts rattling the barn door, pushing rain through the seams, so he and Charlie back deeper into the barn. Charlie's heel clips the handle of an upended bucket, and she tips backwards, landing on a hay bale, flecks of dust and hay fluffing into the air. Charlie's friend's eyes grow wide. Charlie says she's okay, but she already feels her throat closing. She knows what's coming next. He scoops her up in a cradle hold and she wraps her arms around his neck. He kicks open the barn door and ducks into the rain towards the trailer. I'm sorry, Charlie! He glances down and sees her eyes closing, her hair already rain soaked. No, Charlie! Stay awake! Charlie, wake up! His voice sounds so close, so worried, so real. She opens her eyes as he takes the plastic porch steps two at a time and yells,

Patricia! Patricia! She sees her mom peer out a cracked window, annoyed. She disappears from the window and appears at the door. She holds it open with a grimace, glances at Charlie, waves him in. The storm door slams shut behind them against the steel frame as thunder bellows across the trailer park, rattling the windows. Charlie is gasping for air as he lays her on the leather sofa. Mother is rummaging through the kitchen muttering something about how she'll miss her deadline now. He gazes down at Charlie with a sad smile, pushes a stray, damp hair off her forehead. She closes her eyes again. Charlie, wake up, please wake up! She peers at him through swollen eyelids, his eyes so warm; the only person she's ever trusted and would never hurt her. Patricia hands him a red plastic box, then returns to her sewing machine, unconcerned. He flips the lid open and grabs the needle, filling it from the vial. Charlie's vision goes black. Somehow, she still can hear him... Charlie! Charlie! Come on, Charlie! She shivers as thunder shakes the trailer. Charlie. Charlie...

17

Farmhouse Twister

"CHARLIE!" THE VOICE yelled again, tearing her from the blackness.

"Ouch!" Charlie cried, somewhat out of her dream.

Am I still dreaming? No, it's real. And I'm going to die this time.

Wait, did someone just stab me?

The thunder cracked, surging Charlie to fully awake. She opened her eyes and looked up. A man, squatting down over her, held a sharp object in one hand, and her thigh with the other.

James Maynan.

A man accused of serious crimes. Greg had warned her.

And she'd turned on him because James had flirted with her and made her feel seen over a silly conversation about rabbits.

You were right, Greg. I'm so sorry.

"Get off me!" Charlie sat up and shoved James' hands away, reaching for the wound on her thigh. "Where's my briefcase?!"

"Stay still!" James said, pushing her back down. Charlie yelped and pushed him again, harder, knocking him off balance. He fell backwards onto his butt.

"Charlie, stop!" James said, clambering back to his feet, a small grin on his face, a flush on his cheeks. He was taller than she remembered from their diner meeting. Tanned, not fake stuff, but hard, outdoor work where the sun had the benefit of kissing his skin regularly. His sleeves were taut, shoved above his forearms.

"No! I won't... wait. What did you call me?" Charlie paused her struggled and glanced up at him.

James crouched down by Charlie.

"Charlie," James whispered. His expression pleaded with her. Like he wanted her to remember.

What is it, what do you know?

"How do you know my name?" Charlie asked, tears suddenly in her eyes. She thought back to meeting James at the diner. She'd introduced herself as Jane. He'd called her June, twice. Then in the parking lot of the warehouse, the moment they'd shared where nothing else existed. Maybe she'd accidentally said her real name in that temporary world they created.

No, no matter what that was, I didn't tell him my real name.

The man peered at Charlie, his strong arms crossed, looking from the chain to her ankle, to her face.

"What briefcase?" He asked, watching her closely. She felt like she was a beauty queen on stage, and the constant lightning, her spotlight. Despite her fear and confusion, she blushed. She felt hyper aware of how attractive he was. She shook her head.

Get a grip, Charlie! The man kidnapped you!

"You know what I mean, you broke in and stole it!" Charlie said defiantly. She looked down at her hands and realized she was shaking. She jumped as bass-filled thunder joined the sound of the barn door screeching across its rusty nails. A flash of lightning illuminated a tall silhouette in the doorway; a sheet of rain ushered him in.

"Greg!" Charlie cried with relief. "Greg, help me!"

She scrambled backwards away from James as far as her chain would allow, her hand putting pressure on the wound on her thigh. James reached after her, grabbing her right ankle. Greg launched himself across the room, connecting with James across his waist. James huffed as he fell to the floor and Greg landed on top of him. Charlie winced, struggling to scoot away with one hand and a clamped ankle.

"Why are *you* here," Greg hissed to James.

Charlie studied Greg as he stood up. He was panting like he'd just run a mile, wet from the rain, and boiling angry. His lip was bleeding from the bottom. A swollen cheekbone showed signs of recent bruising. Each breath he took raised his shoulders two inches. His shoulders were hunched forward, and his arms hung at his sides away from his body, ready to strike another blow.

Charlie felt a chill crawl down her spine and settle into her bones.

The injuries on his face, I inflicted those. Greg was the masked assailant. Why does he want the briefcase?

"I knew something was wrong when I saw you two at the diner together," James said calmly to Greg. He was still on the floor, his body tense, but ready.

Charlie never felt comfortable around Greg, but he'd never done anything to cause her to distrust him. He was supportive when she lost her fiancé, Tim; she'd been a wreck but had nobody to lean on. Greg stepped up and talked her through many angry midnight outbursts. She'd always appreciated he'd never taken advantage of her vulnerability, never hit on her.

But now, Charlie. Now you know. Trust your instincts!

"Greg...you...how could you..." Charlie tried to say.

"You know why I'm here, Greg. Let Charlie go." James interrupted, breathless. The fall had knocked the wind out of him, and he was taking his time standing up. Charlie could tell he was going slow intentionally, sizing up his situation before moving.

Why is James here, though? And how does he know our names? Charlie thought, watching him. She couldn't stop thinking how attractive he looked, slightly out of breath, lying on the ground ... the rain on the roof ...

Good lord, girl, what is with you! You're tied up on hay

and thinking about a man who just stabbed your thigh.

The rain was coming down with full fury against the roof. Thunder and lightning played a duet in the sky, drowning out the sounds of the wind pushing through the trees.

Never one to rush a fight, Greg hovered a few feet from Charlie, watching James, the veins on his hands prominent from the tight fists positioned firmly at his sides. James shifted his body slightly towards Charlie and she glanced over. Their eyes locked.

Those eyes...

"Charlie," James said. "It's going to be alright."

Charlie caught her breath.

I know that voice...

Charlie hears him yelling her name again, louder, louder. She feels something sharp in her thigh, a slight burn. It's okay, Charlie, you're alright. He smoothes her hair away from her forehead. She can feel a rush of adrenaline from the shot he administered, and then quickly following...air, pure sweet air rushes to heal her lungs. She takes in a deep breath, a few tears fall off the corners of her eyes in relief, feels his fingers swipe the tears away. It's working, Charlie! Opening her heavy eyelids, she sees his face. He's sharing her tears of relief. He says something about avoiding hay from now on. She smiles, studying his gentle face, his soft blue eyes...she trusts him.

"No way," Charlie whispered, staring into familiar eyes. "I remember."

James smiled and she studied his face.

I trust him. How did I not recognize him before?

"Let Charlie go," James repeated, breaking the surreal moment with Charlie. He stood up and calmly faced Greg. "She has nothing to do with this."

Charlie glanced from James to Greg and back again.

They know each other?

Greg's left eye twitched, his shoulders tense.

"What are you talking about?" Greg hesitated, looking around, his voice unsteady. "I'm here to save Charlie."

Greg looked at Charlie with a frown then tossed a key towards her.

"I found this when I tackled James," Greg said

pathetically. He looked defeated but annoyed. The key skittered into the hay pile by Charlie's ankle.

"But you were the one..." Charlie started. "You broke into my room. Why?"

"It wasn't me," Greg responded. He was staring hard at James. James stared back equally intense, both men waiting to see who would make the first move.

"Original, Greg. You almost killed her," James said, his body tense as he pointed at the hay. He looked at Charlie. "Charlie, Greg is ..."

Charlie screeched as Greg leaned in with his right hand and punched James across the jaw, the impact muted as thunder rattled the window.

"Don't you speak, pig," Greg muttered through his teeth, his lungs heaving up and down.

James rubbed his jaw and squared in, nose to nose with Greg. Both men were slick with sweat.

"Gonna take a lot more than that, rich boy," James said, narrowing his eyes at Greg. He inched a little closer. "What are you doing with Charlie? Why did you come back?"

"Greg, James, stop! What is going on?" Charlie asked, the humidity nearly visible in the air. "Get me out of here!"

"Stay out of it!" Greg yelled at Charlie.

Greg shoved into James and James threw a punch. Greg ducked away from it and stepped backwards, moving towards the door. James stepped after him, grabbed his shirt, and yanked him back, slamming a fist into his jaw. Greg moaned and threw his shoulder into James' chest, throwing both off balance and sending them sprawling on the ground.

"What the hell is going on?!" Charlie yelled but her voice was drowned out by the rain on the tin roof.

"The key, Charlie!" James yelled between punches.

"Right!" Charlie nodded and rolled onto her knees, trying not to stir up the hay. With one hand, she searched the floor.

Wait...the hay, Charlie said, connecting her thoughts.

As the boys continued fighting, Charlie lifted a few fingers that were compressing the wound on her thigh and found no blood or knife wound, just a red pin prick dot. She moved her whole hand.

James gave me an EpiPen injection! He saved me, just like before!

"It was an EpiPen!" she said out loud with a smile,

relieved.

That explains why I'm shaking like I'm in an earthquake. Thought I'd gone soft with all this chaos.

James yelled, "Move!" as Greg made a roaring noise out of his throat that sounded like a lion falling off a cliff.

Charlie dove to her left, her chain clattered across the floor, as a moldy partial bale of hay landed where she'd vacated. She glanced back at Greg and saw a maniacal grin on his face. James lunged for him, and they fell to the ground. James pinned Greg on his back and hit him in the face.

Charlie searched hastily for the key as Greg bucked James off and reached for a piece of splintered wood.

There it is!

The key reflected a bolt of lightning. She heard James groan as she snatched the key off the wooden floor.

Suddenly, silence.

No wind.

No thunder.

No rain.

Nothing.

James and Greg stood up, both bleeding from various

injuries on their faces, arms, and fists. Everybody looked at the roof at the same time.

The silence was deafening.

"My ears are popping," Charlie said, looking at James with wide eyes.

"We have to go. *Now!*" James started to run towards Charlie, looking at her ankle.

"No!" Greg lunged at James and knocked him to the ground. Charlie unlocked her ankle cuff and stood up, the adrenaline dose from the EpiPen coursing through her body.

Taking a kick to the gut, Greg folded over moaning. James followed Charlie as she ran for the door.

"Do you smell that?" Charlie yelled to James worriedly as she ran outside through the barn door. The smell of freshly cut wood hung in the air. Just as fast as it had stopped, the rain began in sheets and the lightning reached for the treetops, the thunder came in tumultuous waves.

James nodded, looking behind them at a black sky.

"The farmhouse should have a basement!" Charlie pointed to an aged farmhouse across an overgrown field.

James grabbed her hand and started running down the hill away from the storm.

The noise of the storm was deafening. Charlie didn't know if it sounded more like a sawmill, a quarry, or a freight train. Halfway to the house, Charlie felt a stinging pain on her right arm. She slowed for a second and glanced down. Blood. The cut was close to the surface, but bleeding heavily.

"Is that a piece of a tree in your arm?" James asked incredulously. Glancing behind them, he ducked as a branch soared through the air. "It's right behind us! Go!"

They approached the farmhouse at full speed and leapt onto the wooden wrap-around porch. Charlie glanced back and saw the barn disintegrate into a billion toothpicks; her soaked hair pasted across her cheek. James kicked opened the front door.

"Greg!" Charlie looked back one last time.

"No time, Charlie. Inside!" James yelled over the wind.

Charlie rushed in as the first of the barn debris peppered the house, small knives made of timber.

"Over here! The basement!" Charlie led James through the quivering house. "The house is going to go any moment!"

Charlie and James ran down the basement stairs three at a time and dove into the corner as the entire first floor lifted off the house into the angry, swirling sky. James pushed Charlie further into the corner and covered her with his body, his hands interlaced around her head. Charlie covered her ears with her hands.

"Oh, Greg!" Charlie cried. James made a noise in the back of his throat and scrunched his face in disgust.

"Look out!"

The roof smashed back down on the house, showering them with glass shards and smashed bricks. James leaned into Charlie harder, protecting her from the onslaught. She felt the heat from his body.

"Argh!" he moaned as the debris landed on his exposed back.

"Are you okay?" Charlie yelled.

James nodded grimly. Charlie took her hands off her ears and reached around him like a hug, her face inches from his. Looking into his blue eyes, she could feel his breath. She cleared the debris off his back, brushed his hair off his forehead.

James gazed back at her as the thunder slowed, the sky quieted. The humidity dissipated, and a refreshing rain took over the sky.

"It's almost over, Charlie," James assured.

"I trust you," Charlie said quietly.

Leaning in closer, Charlie put her hands on James' face and pressed her lips to his.

18

Clarity

THE RAIN CONTINUED to wash across the scarred terrain, as if Mother Nature were apologizing for her angry outburst. Charlie and James worked methodically to unbury themselves from the basement, dodging rusty nails, plaster chunks, brick shards, and electrical wires. The stairs were destroyed and climbing the foundation wall was the only option to escape.

"Remember the day we were playing in Jack Brown's field when that storm hit, and we ran into the barn?" Charlie asked, ducking under a wire that James held up.

"Yeah. Definitely. I couldn't tell if your mother was more angry we were hanging out or that you were nearly dead.

I kicked myself for years after that. I knew you were allergic to hay. Jack knew, too, and warned us so many times to avoid that barn. Two days later you and your mom vanished," James said with a sad frown. He squatted down on one knee and laced his fingers together to make a footstep. "Here, I think we've cleared enough to be safe over here. Let me try to boost you up."

Charlie put her left hand on James' shoulder then lifted his chin towards her with her right hand.

"Don't blame yourself. You were the only bright spot in my childhood," Charlie said smiling down at him. "You saved me in so many ways. You looked out for me when I had nobody else. I can't believe I didn't recognize you when I saw you at the diner."

"I was shocked to see you. And then you said your name was Jane," James smiled curiously. "But those curls, they gave you away. You grew up well."

Laughing, Charlie blushed and released his chin. She put her right foot in his waiting hands. Taking a deep breath, she leaned into James, and he lifted her up with ease. She couldn't help but admire his arms.

And to think, my best childhood friend, James, is the big

bad guy I am after in this case.

Charlie smiled as she looked away and scurried up the final level of foundation. She sat on the edge of the wall surrounded by broken wooden boards. Looking around, she said, "I remember pretty much nothing about life here, James. Pieces come in nightmares and sometimes a sound will throw me into a broken memory, but that's all." Charlie looked down at James. "Whose house was this? How did you know where I was? Or that I was in trouble?"

James grunted as he climbed the foundation wall. A moment later he was sitting next to Charlie on the crumbling embankment. They were both drenched from the rain and Charlie's arm was still bleeding from the wooden shard that hit her as she ran away from the tornado. James' shirt was torn in multiple spaces across his shoulders and little red drops of blood oozed from various cuts.

"I never expected you to return here, Charlie," James began. He searched her eyes as he spoke. "I knew you'd joined the FBI and worked out of the Albany office. Seeing you a few days ago threw me off, especially when the sheriff's office told me that a homemade bomb is what leveled my records office. You just happen to show up right before it happened."

"I didn't know this was my hometown when I accepted the case I'm on. I'm in a weird position now. I will probably ask to be removed from the case since it's become...personal," Charlie said with a bit of relief.

"Personal? I figured since you were using a false name you were on a case. After I saw you and Greg at the diner, Debra told me she felt you were in danger and mentioned your mother used to work at Tina's and how surprised you'd been at that discovery. I realized then you were either trying to continue your cover, or you didn't remember. This morning, Debra called and said she was worried about you after the guy you were with was being unusually rude."

James stood up and reached out for Charlie's hand. He gestured around him.

"This is Greg's family home," James continued. "Figured if Greg was up to something he'd go somewhere familiar. The house has been vacant for over a decade, though."

Charlie grabbed his hand and allowed him to pull her to standing. Smiling still, she felt intoxicated by his presence. It was easy in this moment to forget about Greg, the monumental pile of answers she needed, or the fact that she'd just survived a tornado.

Can I just get lost in his eyes and forget Greg, Mother, and the case? Charlie wished. She felt like every answer she received confused her even more.

"Greg lived here?" Charlie asked, bewildered.

"Yes, but the question remains of why he is back," James said, scrunching his eyebrows as if solving a challenging math problem in his head. He looked around again.

"James, we were childhood friends, I remember that now. Why did you hang out with a boring five-year-old?" Charlie held his hand tight, feeling every heartbeat between their fingers.

James smiled and turned his body to face Charlie. He reached out and grabbed her other hand.

"Charlie, you deserved so much more than you were given. Your dad adored you; protected you from your mother. When Hank died, Patricia went seriously off the rails for a while. I may have been young, but I knew you needed someone to look out for you. My dad, Peter, filed a custody petition with the court; tried to make a case to take you into our home. Your mom found out and left town with you and essentially disappeared for years. Patricia came back about fifteen years later—she'd cleaned herself up—and then felt the need to keep me updated with your whereabouts." James brushed a curl off Charlie's cheek.

"I didn't allow communication from my mom once I left home," Charlie shrugged feeling sad, wondering what life would have been like with a normal mother. "And I didn't know she kept tabs on me. I figured she was happy to be free of me. Can't believe your dad tried to do that for me. I saw a news article that he passed away young, too. I'm sorry."

James nodded appreciatively.

"And I don't understand what happened to my dad," Charlie continued covering her face with her hands. She was fighting back tears. She told herself it was just the adrenaline wearing off, but she knew she was opening scars she'd bandaged a long time ago. Dropping her hands, she glanced up at James. His steady gaze encouraged her to continue. "Or honestly much of anything yet. Mother never let me talk about my dad.

She'd flat out get violent. It's been a confusing few days here."

"He was a good man," James said with a sigh. He brushed another curl away from Charlie's face and rubbed the back of his finger across her cheek. "I don't know what you remember or not, so ask away. But for now, we should start making our way back to town; it's a hike from here. We need to get cleaned up and find out what Greg is up to."

Charlie nodded, gathering herself. She smiled up at James; a silent thank you.

Right, Greg. Charlie felt she should be concerned or go looking for Greg. But she didn't feel inclined to. She had so many questions jumping around her head she couldn't seem to grab just one.

As if he sensed her internal fight, James squeezed her hand and then looked around again. Eventually his eyes rested on a newer blue pickup truck. The tornado had rolled the truck onto its side then dropped a large tree trunk onto it. The truck appeared to be severed in half.

"Ahh, there it is. Man, that is certainly not where I left it." Still holding Charlie's hand, James picked his way through the debris-filled driveway toward the heavily damaged truck. He crouched down and peered through the cracked windshield, looking for anything to salvage.

"I don't see the CrownVic, so I guess Greg survived? Or perhaps the car is in the neighbor's house," Charlie said half-joking but still wondering how much she should care about Greg's demise. "Wait, how do you know him, anyways?"

James stood up and looked at Charlie in surprise, one hand resting on the bent door frame.

"You seriously don't know who he is to you?" James said.

"Know who Greg is? He's my partner at the Bureau. Been in the Albany office for about two years. Before that he was in Buffalo, and Baltimore, I think," Charlie said with a shrug. She leaned back slightly as she felt James' stare land heavily on her. "Why are you looking at me like that?"

James shook his head still looking at her in shock.

"Charlie, Greg is your cousin," James said throwing his right hand in the air. "His dad, Lester, killed your dad and himself in a fight at the warehouse. You didn't know this? Greg is a loose cannon. Nearly killed his mother a few years ago."

Charlie couldn't speak. She felt weak. Her mind raced through all her interactions with Greg. All the times she felt something was wrong; knew something was off about him. How he showed up right after Tim's death and sometimes still casually asks if any clues have come up. The call with Jessica about a "tip that Greg blackmailed his way into the FBI." The low jack on her Rabbit. One car for this assignment. Debra's warning. How she had considered kissing him just a handful of days ago. The motel break-in. The fight between James and Greg in the barn. And then...

Charlie's mouth fell open as she recalled the final words Mother left on the answering machine:

Look out for your cousin, Charlie.

19

Greg in the Light

"BUT HOW IS he my partner, then? The Bureau doesn't allow familial partners," Charlie sputtered. She had reached a point where her thoughts were falling over each other, and she couldn't focus on any one thing. She started pacing a small path, three steps forward, spin around, three steps forward. "No, I didn't know Greg was my cousin. He's Greg *Hamlin* not *Winslow*. Anyways, why did Mother warn me about him? Why didn't she just say, 'Hey, kiddo, look out for Greg; he's dangerous'. No! Instead, the message was all cryptic, as if I were to find him to play a game of cards or share some eggs. On top of that, if his dad killed my dad, what does Greg want with *me*?

Shouldn't it be the other way around?" She threw her hands up in the air and sputtered a few indiscernible words.

James grunted as he pulled the shattered glass of the pickup passenger side window out piece by piece and tossed them aside. Once the glass surrounding the space was cleared, he reached in and opened the glove box, pulling out a first aid kit.

"Come here, Charlie. Stop pacing. I need to stop the bleeding from your arm," James said. His eyes looked slightly amused at her irritation, but his smile was gentle. He reached his arms out showing a bandage and an alcohol wipe as if to wave a white flag of neutrality.

Charlie stopped pacing and with one glance at James, temporarily forgot why she was mad.

Why does he look like he's asking me to come to bed with him and why am I inclined to say yes?

Charlie gave in and walked back over to James, dodging the recently discarded glass shards. She reached her bleeding arm out towards James' healing hands and let out a loud sigh.

"I guess I need to call Jessica—she's my main contact at

the Albany field office —and let her know my partner kidnapped me and tied me up in a barn. She will probably send out a team or two to find him," Charlie said, trying to find the tough agent side of her brain. She worked to calm her mind and focus on next steps. She needed to find Greg, and make sure he didn't hurt anybody else. She also needed answers.

Charlie watched James' hands work. She concluded that his fingers were electrical circuits; little shocks coursed between their hands from every whispering touch. She couldn't tell if he noticed, but she thought about kissing him again.

You're just feeling vulnerable, stay focused, Charlie told herself.

But she knew her desire to kiss him wasn't because her world was falling apart; she was attracted to James and he to her. She could feel it. And she felt *safe*.

With his smile fulfilling its gentle promise, James cleaned the area around her cut and talked about running his warehouse while he placed butterfly bandages across the open wound. His voice soothed her nerves, and she felt her mind start to take back control.

"Like I said earlier, your mom eventually cleaned herself up and came back," James said, eyeing Charlie with a pleading expression. "She knew you wanted nothing to do with her and accepted that." He nodded as if deciding on some resolution, then continued. "A few years ago, she got a call from Greg's mom, Janet. They hadn't talked in years because when Janet found out what Lester had done, she'd taken Greg, who was only three, and left town, eventually marrying into a wealthy, heavily influential family. Greg grew up a rich kid with a chip on his shoulder thinking his mom's husband was his birth-dad. Greg used his dad's name, Hamlin, to get into any club, party, or job he wanted—taking full advantage of the family name his mom married into." James paused to check his work with the bandages and then nodded again, this time in self-approval.

"That explains why he always acts like a shallow frat boy. Girls fall all over him. It's gross." Charlie shook her head. Just talking about Greg put a sour taste in her mouth. "So, he found a way to get into the FBI. And clearly targeted me. Two years ago, my partner unexpectedly retired, and Greg replaced him. Two months later, my fiancé," Charlie looked James in the eye, "was murdered. No clues were found and nobody was charged. I wonder if Greg..."

James frowned.

"I'm sorry to hear that, Charlie. That must feel awful. I don't know Greg personally, but I bet he's capable of murder. After all, you almost died today."

Charlie felt a chill on her skin. Shaking her head, she pushed the thought of Greg killing Tim out of her head.

Can't think about that right now, Charlie told herself.

"I know Greg; he's skilled at surviving," Charlie said to James. "If the CrownVic isn't here, he somehow got out of that barn and ran." She reached for the first aid items then set them on a branch by James' back. "Here, my turn. You have a few scrapes on your shoulders that are still bleeding."

James took off his rain-soaked, torn t-shirt. Charlie sucked in a quick breath and stared at his bare, strong shoulders.

Focus, Charlie...not the time or place for these thoughts!

Despite her internal argument, Charlie allowed herself an appreciative grin as she knelt behind him.

"Any idea why he chose the FBI? He's been in for years,

only two with me," Charlie repeated. "If he wanted to get back at me, couldn't he have just found where I lived and killed me or something?"

James shrugged.

"I didn't think anything of it until I saw you here, but I wouldn't be surprised if he's trying to sabotage your career or just toy with your life. You know, the barn and what not," James said, trailing off.

Charlie flashed back to the hay itching her arms and the chain chaffing her ankle. She could feel her lungs resisting air, the panic just a breath away.

What does *Greg want with me? Does he really want to kill me? Did he kill Tim?*

Charlie felt herself lean into James' bare chest. He was warm, solid, safe. James wrapped his arms around her and held her tightly. He didn't ask, didn't push her away, didn't demand an explanation. He breathed in and out. The rhythm soothed her.

Since when do I ask for a hug?

Charlie realized what she'd done and looked into his face. His gaze was calm, patient. He was following her lead.

"Um, so what did Aunt Janet call Mother for?" Charlie

asked, reaching once again for the first aid kit. She began with the larger cut on his left upper shoulder. His skin was warm and soft. She gently dabbed around the wound then laid the bandage.

"Well, unfortunately for Janet, she loved wine," James snorted. "One night she got drunk and told Greg about what Lester—Greg's real dad—had done. Janet told Greg his dad had started showing signs of mania in his mid-thirties and she was worried Greg might be heading that direction, too. She wanted Greg to see a specialist for preventative help. I guess Greg got so angry he beat her up bad then took off and she hadn't seen him in months and was worried about him. She called Patricia to see if she'd seen Greg."

"Who beats up their own mother?" Charlie asked in disgust. "Although I may have considered it a time or two, I suppose. Anyways, this is the best I can do while it's still raining." She patted his shoulder, trying to force the bandages to stick. Feeling his muscles move under her hand, she allowed her hand to linger a moment longer than necessary.

Charlie took a breath and forced her hand to move. She

picked up his t-shirt intending to hand it to him. The previously blue t-shirt was soaked through, torn, and blood-stained. She held the t-shirt up in the air and James turned around.

"Uhh, probably not worth putting back on," Charlie said with what she felt was a silly grin, but she couldn't stop.

Pull yourself together, Charlie! You are better at controlling your emotions during a sting operation than during a basic conversation with this man. Even if he is a very attractive, strong man with no shirt. And the way the rain is streaming off his chest...stop!

"Wouldn't say your shirt is in any better condition if you care to be even," James said with a sly smile gesturing towards Charlie.

Charlie looked down in horror. Her light pink blouse was completely see-through due to the rain and the seam on the right had a trail of blood down to the hem. Several of the buttons were missing and her heather grey sports bra was on full display. She couldn't help but laugh.

"This has been the weirdest day of my life," Charlie said. "We need to get to a phone. I must warn Jessica about Greg. She was right all along."

"Let's start walking towards town," James said. He stood and reached for Charlie's hand with a soft smile.

Guess I'm not the only one appreciating the best out of this situation, Charlie thought. She felt like the prettiest human alive when he looked at her, his brows slightly furrowed. His gaze was gentle, protective. She reached out and placed her hand in his. A moment or two passed as she admired the feeling of fireworks launching from both of them.

James pulled her hand toward him, reaching his other hand up to her hair. He played with a curl on her forehead then traced a raindrop down her cheek. He hooked his finger under her chin and pulled her closer. Leaning down he pressed his lips against hers.

"We'll find Greg, Charlie," James assured Charlie.

The rain stopped and Charlie felt like the temperature had risen seventeen degrees. She leaned into his kiss, tasting him and the rain. She felt more connected to James and this moment than she had ever felt at any point in her life. He kissed her deeply then leaned back and smiled down at her.

"You're safe, Charlie," James said sincerely. A pained

look spread across his face as he choked out, "Will you leave again?"

Charlie felt her insides twist. She wanted to tell him she was never leaving his side. That she'd give up everything for him.

But who does that? I have a career, a house, a garden. He has his business. I hardly know this man.

Charlie felt as sad as James looked but she knew deep down, she would never be able to say goodbye. She searched his eyes for the right answer. Before she could speak, the sound of an approaching engine forced them both to look away. A horn honked.

"That looks like Debra's minivan," James said, disappointed. He stepped back a pace but kept her hand in his.

Charlie reminded herself to breathe; she didn't want this moment to end. She squeezed James' hand in acknowledgment to his question; a promise to revisit the question. She waved at Debra as the minivan came to a stop. Charlie still felt the rush of James' kiss and reflected his disappointed expression.

"Hey! I'm so glad to see you're both okay!" Debra

exclaimed. She came out of the van like a missile and beelined for Charlie, her normally perfect blonde ponytail askew. Gently squeezing shoulders, Debra pushed Charlie back and glanced up and down. "I would have come sooner but we were all in the community shelter. Had to help a few of the older folks home. Charlie, oh, but...do you want a shirt? I think I have a sweatshirt in the van."

Charlie chuckled and tugged on the bottom seam of her destroyed shirt.

"You don't like my new style?" Charlie knew that in another life, her and Debra would be lifelong friends.

Maybe we can still in this life.

"Oops, yes. I just hope this phase ends soon. I'll respect it for now, though," Debra said with a full smile. Her smile faded as she looked around, noting the missing barn and the flattened house. "But, for real. Are you guys okay? Looks like you went through the real weather. What a storm! Fortunately, the twister missed the main part of town."

Charlie glanced at James and realized he'd never looked away. He smiled and squeezed her hand. She felt euphoric, but knew from training, it was probably just adrenaline and would wear off in a few hours.

Please don't wear off. I love this feeling.

"Yeah, we're okay, Debra," Charlie said reaching out to hug Debra. "Thanks for coming to get us. I was not looking forward to that walk back. I'm glad you're okay, too! How did you know where we were?"

Debra turned towards the minivan and waved James and Charlie to follow.

"I hope you're not mad," Debra said, "but I told James I was worried about you when I didn't see you for several meals and he told me your true identity." She glanced back sheepishly at Charlie as she opened the driver's door.

James held open the front passenger door for Charlie then he climbed in the back of the van. Charlie's hand felt cold when James released her hand.

Charlie settled into the passenger seat and smiled over at Debra.

"It's alright," Charlie assured Debra, patting her leg. "I'm sorry I had to lie to you about who I was. I usually don't mind, but for you two, it was different. Never a good part of my job," Charlie replied and glanced between Debra then back at James.

Debra smiled back then started the van. She shifted into drive and guided the van to the road, dodging tree branches and various pieces of barn and housing materials.

Greg survived. I can feel it.

"After what happened with your coworker earlier today, I called James. I know I'd told you to be careful, but it wasn't enough. James met me at Tina's Cafe," Debra continued. "One of our older regulars, Billy, overheard us talking and mentioned he'd seen a car trespassing on the Winslow property. I swear James turned a whole new shade of red when he heard that. He started going off about hay and allergies and Charlie this and Charlie that. You remember my son, Oliver, he's allergic to strawberries, so I carry an EpiPen. James grabbed it when I held it out and took off without another word. Then the storm hit, and I had to wait to follow him."

Charlie nodded then looked at James.

"He certainly came at the right time. Thank you, both," Charlie said smiling at James. "I'd have either died from the hay or the tornado or both." The three fell into silence for a moment as each imagined the possible outcomes.

"When I first met you, Debra, you'd mentioned there was an accident at the warehouse. James, can you tell me more about my dad's death?" Charlie asked.

James cleared his throat.

"Here's what I know," James said. "That event in the warehouse wasn't an accident as the newspaper claimed. Lester, Greg's dad, tried to kill both Peter, my dad, and Hank, your dad, so he could take over the company. Tucker, your grandpa, who started the company, shipped illegal stuff for various clients, always finding a way to hide it from weight reports and border inspections."

"He shipped illegal stuff?" Charlie asked. She desperately wanted to tell James the real reason she was in town but felt bound by the fact she was an FBI agent on an official case.

Is my grandpa the start of this whole case? Who tipped off the FBI?

"Yeah, but wait," James continued. "When Tucker died in 1960, Hank, Lester, and Peter—two of his kids and their closest friend—took over. Hank and Peter methodically rid the company of the illegal activities, which naturally lowered profits. Lester didn't like that. He hoped by ridding himself of his brother and Peter, he'd be able to bring back the illegal profits. He staged an accident in a secluded part of the warehouse. Unfortunately, he underestimated Peter. Lester shot Hank in the leg after a scuffle and turned to shoot Peter. Peter ducked and tackled Lester around the waist. The two fought over the gun, Peter eventually gaining control and he tried to just shoot Lester in the shoulder to disable him. Unfortunately, he got too close to the heart and Lester died instantly. Hank made it a couple hours, but the bullet grazed a major vein, and the doctors couldn't repair it fast enough in surgery."

"Wow," Charlie said digesting the image of her dad dying during surgery. "So, Greg is probably avenging his father's death, and he was mad when James found me, because he knew you'd protect me."

Charlie felt part of a stomach knot release. Some things were starting to make sense. She realized if James were to protect himself, and possibly her, he needed all the information. If she got fired for sharing, so be it.

"So, I feel like I can say this now, but I'm here because 'a credible source' tipped the FBI that Tucker Trucking and

Company was part of illegal shipping over the border. I'm supposed to be here as no-contact, observation only. Greg also told me that James may be connected with a few murders."

"That's absurd," Debra said with a grunt. "James and his company support the community, and we haven't had a murder for fourteen years!"

"Well, then we know who the 'credible source' was, don't we?" James offered.

Greg. He's been playing me for years. How did I not see this?

You did, Charlie, a voice said. *You always knew.*

"We're both drenched. Debra," James piped up," would you mind dropping me off at the warehouse and then get Charlie back to the motel?"

"No problem at all," Debra replied stealing a glance at James in the rearview mirror. She seemed to be appreciating his shirtless style, too.

"That's a good idea. Thank you," Charlie said. "I'll call the field office and then clean my arm up a little more. Can I meet you back at the warehouse after?"

"For sure," James said.

Charlie turned around and looked at James. He had his left arm draped across the back of the car seat bench. His knees were spread apart comfortably and his eyes surveyed the landscape as it passed outside his window. He appeared calm and in control, not like he hadn't just been in a fist fight, ran from a tornado, and saved an old friend from death. Charlie could see his upper body was drying off, but water still dripped from his dark hair. She admired the little ringlets of hair that were beginning to form around his ears and neck. She'd always wished her curls were tighter but had learned to love her wavy curls.

James turned his head forward and their eyes locked. His blue eyes captivated her gaze, and she felt goosebumps take over her arms. She jumped when Debra spoke, breaking the spell his eyes had cast.

"Here we are," Debra chuckled quietly and looked at Charlie with a little smile. Charlie suddenly felt slightly embarrassed and wondered if Debra and James were a thing or had ever been. She'd heard James mention a Bill but wasn't sure if that was Debra's significant other or an inside joke.

The minivan pulled into the dirt lot by the warehouse

and came to a stop. The records office was still a pile of rubble but no longer smoking. Yellow lines of ribbon surrounded the concrete and brick stack.

"I'll stay with Charlie and bring her back when she's ready," Debra said with a sincere glance at James.

James climbed out of the van and shut the door then stood next to the passenger window. Charlie rolled the window down and leaned both her elbows on the door. She tilted her head up towards James with a content smile.

"Why don't you check out of the motel and stay here until we find Greg," James said, his gaze hard, protective.

"At the warehouse?" Charlie asked looking behind James at the large, metal building.

"Actually, my house is up the hill behind the warehouse," James said with a grin, pointing to the left. "But I'm sure I can find you a spare wooden pallet if you'd prefer the warehouse."

"Oh, that would make more sense," Charlie said with a grunt and jokingly shoved James' shoulder. "Thanks, I would like that."

I would love *that. Out of this storm, can I find happiness? Am I capable of merging my past and my future?*

James smiled as if he didn't already know she'd say yes and tapped the top of the car. He waved goodbye with an excited smile as Charlie rolled up the window and Debra pulled out of the lot.

"Well, that was some serious heat between you two," Debra said slyly.

Charlie glanced over, unsure what Debra's tone implied. Debra had a huge smile on her face, and her eyes were shining with amusement. Charlie relaxed.

"It did feel a little intense. It's funny seeing someone after this long and experiencing completely different emotions. I'm not...you two aren't... dating or anything, right? I mean, I'm not trying to cause any problems," Charlie stammered and shivered, suddenly feeling the chill of her damp clothes.

I wish James were here to warm me up.

"Goodness, no," Debra said shaking her head, giggling. "I've known James a long time, but I'm happily married. My husband, Bill, works for James as a driver." She smiled at Charlie. "James is all yours."

James is all yours.

"He's not seeing anybody else?" Charlie cringed at asking such a girly question, but she was *not* a home wrecker.

Debra laughed again, her smile dazzling the windshield. She was clearly enjoying the real-life soap opera.

"I am not sure I've ever seen James get serious with another girl, save from one back in our early twenties. That lasted about a year or two then she moved away to the big city and found another man. She has like three kids now. James honestly didn't seem to mind her leaving. Almost like he was waiting for somebody," Debra glanced over at Charlie with a half grin.

Charlie fell silent and gazed out the window as the tree-lined driveways swept by. It felt weird to her how calm she felt when she thought about James.

He could be mine, she repeated. *He knows who I am, and everything I've been through. I don't have to explain anything to him or hope he understands. And it is easy being with him.*

The only other time she'd considered being with a man she had to mantra herself repeatedly that it was normal to find someone eventually and settle down. When she met

Tim, she knew he was safe and that he loved her. That had been enough for Charlie. She thought at the time he was all she needed.

Finding Tim murdered had hurt and driven her to fall even deeper into her personal emotional prison. She cared for Tim; but she knew now, in this moment, she hadn't truly loved him. Her love for him had been convenience and cliche—a feeling she thought she had to create. A requirement of getting older. Find somebody that won't add to your pain and settle down—that's enough.

Guilt pained her stomach.

He's gone, Charlie, she reminded herself. *You don't have to feel guilty. It's okay...you know now he wouldn't have been enough for you nor you for him and both of us would have figured it out in a year or two of marriage and then gone our separate ways.*

And yet she'd fallen completely for James in just a few minutes. Or perhaps she'd already loved him from her childhood. She trusted him with no questions. She *felt* it. Charlie no longer felt the shame or burden of her childhood. James didn't stare at her with pity; didn't see her as a broken human. He saw her as she was now and yet knew the little girl he protected so many years ago.

Charlie closed her eyes replaying their kiss in the rain; the way his hand felt holding hers. A light smile played on her lips.

And he asked me to stay. Didn't ask where I'd been. He already knows.

Charlie made a noise somewhere between a groan, a sob, and a chuckle. Debra glanced over at her with a concern held between her eyebrows.

"Sorry," Charlie said taking a deep breath. "Last time I got close to someone he was murdered. Two years later and still no leads. Perhaps even by Greg's hand." Charlie moaned again in pain as she finally allowed the image of Greg pointing the gun at Tim to pass through her vision.

Debra's jaw dropped. "Charlie that is awful!"

"It was a weird time. I'd finally agreed to marry someone—which was hard. It was at the same time my partner of years randomly retired and Greg—the guy I've been with here and you know as Paul—was transferred in." Charlie didn't like the timing and how Greg's motive was adding up.

I have to find out Greg's next move! Now I know how

he drove here without a map...he already knew this place! So somehow coming to Old Mill was part of his plan, but based on his mood since we've arrived, it's not going to plan.

"So, Greg is your cousin, huh?" Debra asked, as if she were chartering Charlie's current state of mind.

"Apparently," Charlie said matter of fact.

"Um, that's kind of gross. I heard about the diner and dancing drama a couple weeks ago. I thought maybe you two were falling for each other or something romantic like that. Sorry, small towns."

Charlie shuddered at the thought and again chastised herself for even considering kissing him that night.

"I still don't know how to process it. Greg showed up randomly two years ago and has been at my side since. He showed up right before Tim was murdered. They didn't get along, but it didn't matter; I kept work and home separate." Charlie shook her head.

No matter how much she distrusted Greg, she never thought him capable of murder.

Charlie told Debra about the barn, running from the tornado, and the kiss in the basement.

"Like I said, heat," Debra said with a smile. "Any further into this story and I might swoon!"

Charlie laughed.

"Debra, when we get to the motel, I need to get into Greg's assigned motel room. He disappeared after the tornado, and I need to see if there's any sign of where he might have gone. I'm not sure he ever used that room. Perhaps he's been staying at that old house this whole time."

"Can I help?" Debra grinned and began drumming the steering wheel.

Charlie glanced at Debra and saw her smile.

"I get excited before a big break, too, Debra. But don't let your guard down easily. Greg is a trained assassin and clearly has some massive vendetta. Be careful."

"I understand," Debra said with a temporary stern expression. As fast as she spoke, her smile and drumming returned.

"Okay you can help me. But then, I *really* need dry clothes," Charlie replied with a nod, expecting Debra to ask a million follow-up questions.

"Yes! Adventure, here we come!" Debra said instead.

She saluted the air as the speedometer crept higher.

Charlie smiled gratefully over at Debra.

For the second time in one day, Charlie found herself trusting another human.

20

Contemplation

BY THE TIME Charlie and Debra pulled up to the motel, they had devised a plan. Debra was to pose as "Paul's" wife and tell the front desk he'd been in an accident and she needed to clear out his room. She'd get a key, and Charlie would meet her by the room. Knowing how flirty the front desk attendant could be, Charlie had no doubt that Debra's blonde hair would catch his attention.

Charlie verified Greg's CrownVic was nowhere to be seen in the parking lot as Debra parked the minivan. Debra stopped to fluff her hair and adjust her bra before strutting into the lobby, taking on the persona of a saddened debutant perfectly. Charlie was amused at her new friend's dramatic flair but felt apprehensive. Her mind was beginning to process all she'd learned about her family, about James, and Greg, and the cut on her arm was bleeding profusely. Opening the glove box, Charlie found some fast-food napkins with an "M" emblazoned in the paper and wrapped it around her arm, trying to seal off the cut.

As quickly as she'd entered, Debra skipped out of the lobby with a satisfied smile and held the key up just enough for Charlie to see. Charlie nodded and Debra turned back in and walked through the lobby toward the room. Charlie exited the minivan and entered through the side entrance. Then followed Debra, at a distance, to room 311.

"Nice work!" Charlie said quietly once she caught up to Debra by Greg's door. "Can only imagine what you did to get that key."

Debra blushed and looked down then back at Charlie.

"Nothing too inappropriate," Debra replied with a side smile.

"Ha, well it worked," Charlie said. She smiled at Debra to let her know she appreciated her. "Let me go in first, in case he is still in there."

Debra nodded silently and handed Charlie the key. Charlie noted Debra looked proud of herself and made a mental note to tell Debra later that she would have made a great agent in the FBI.

Taking a breath, Charlie turned the key in the lock.

"I could so get fired for this," she whispered to Debra. "Although, after all this, maybe I'll quit."

Debra responded with a nonchalant shrug.

Charlie gently pushed the door open with her left hand, hoping for no rusty hinges. The door opened easily and soundlessly. Charlie signaled Debra to hold the spring hinged door open and wait and then stepped into the room holding her breath.

Light-blocking curtains were drawn closed. The room was completely dark, with a sense of vacancy hanging in the air. Charlie glanced into the bathroom to the right and then moved deeper into the dark room. Every one of Charlie's senses told her there was nobody here. Nonetheless, she tiptoed to the edge of the double bed on the right and leaned forward to check the far side of the bed.

The door behind Charlie slammed shut; a jarring wood-on-metal clatter echoed through the room.

Charlie spun around.

"Someone was coming down the hallway. I panicked. I'm sorry," Debra said sheepishly from somewhere near the door.

Charlie shook her head only slightly annoyed and walked over to a shadow of a lamp. She reached under the shade and flipped the light on. Yellowish light flooded the room. She glanced back.

Debra stood by the door with an apologetic smile and shrugged again.

A slight tap on the door interrupted further investigation.

Charlie gestured at Debra and the door.

"Oh, uh...yes?" Debra said to the door.

"Ma'am, just checking to make sure you're alright. Do you need any assistance?"

That horny desk attendant, Charlie thought.

Debra looked at Charlie like she was about to laugh until she fell to the ground. Charlie shoved her hands toward Debra, signaling her to get rid of him, then put her finger over her lips.

"You know, I'd rather just work through this alone, I'm sure you understand," Debra said, managing to sound sad rather than amused.

"Of course, my mistake. You know where I am if you need me," the attendant replied, sounding disappointed. His footsteps echoed through the hallway as he made his way back to the emergency exit stairs.

"Well, I underestimated the nuisance level of that one," Charlie said, fully annoyed.

Debra finally allowed the giggles to take over and soon tears were slipping down her cheeks.

"I'm sorry," Debra said between giggles, "that kid was so easy to play. I only focused on making sure I got the key I didn't think he'd follow me up here. I'd be a terrible agent!" She took deep breaths to control herself.

"Fortunately, nobody is in here," Charlie said. Then she looked around bewildered, refocused on her task. "Maybe never been here?"

Gesturing Debra to come further into the room, Charlie noticed there were no suitcases or clothes, and the bed was freshly made. She walked over to the bathroom and switched on the light. A dying exhaust fan above the toilet turned on, its metal blades scraping the ceiling. After a short delay, a yellow light bulb above the vanity flickered on, then off again.

"Lovely," Charlie said glaring at the exhaust fan. Turning off the switch, she walked back into the room shaking her head. "No toiletries; no sign of anybody having been here!"

"This is like every movie I've ever loved," Debra said, clearly enjoying the suspense. "What is it you're looking for, anyways?"

"A briefcase, for starters," Charlie answered, still confused on where Greg's personal effects were.

Has he been staying at the decrepit farmhouse this whole time? That would explain why he didn't stop at his room when I listened to him walk away the other night.

"Okay, but we need to get your arm bandage replaced soon. You're bleeding everywhere," Debra said, pointing to Charlie's wound that was now leaking blood through the thin napkins Charlie found in the minivan.

"Ugh, okay," Charlie said not wanting to look at her arm. "Do you think I need stitches?"

Emma Brattin

Debra stepped closer and gently lifted Charlie's arm. She peered under the soddy napkins for a moment.

"No, I don't," Debra decided confidently. "But it certainly needs to be cleaned and properly bandaged."

Debra released Charlie's arm then walked across the room towards the black out curtains. Charlie smiled at Debra's gentleness. This woman barely knew her, discovered she'd been lying, and still was there in a dangerous moment to help her out.

I need more people like her in my life, Charlie decided.

"What is this briefcase anyways? Got top secret FBI-like files in there? Afraid they'll get into the wrong hands? I mean, breaking and entering is a big deal, must be important," Debra asked as she went through the aged oak desk drawers.

"Without going into a whole thing," Charlie dropped to her knees and crawled around on the floor, looking under furniture, "the briefcase was left here by my mother, Patricia, in hopes I'd come seek it out eventually. Greg broke into my room, knocked me out, stole the suitcase, then kidnapped me and tied me up in a barn."

Debra glanced over at Charlie.

"I know I'm all peppy and having fun," Debra said with a soft smile, "but that's a lot. I'm sorry. How are you so calm? I never mean to pry, but it was shocking to see how much you looked like that photo at the diner. And the fact you had no idea…" Debra moved away from the desk and opened the closet door, rattling wooden hangers together.

"I've been in the FBI for a long time. My cases are *always* dangerous, weird, and painful. But this time, I'm digging up past moments I had forgotten and I'm not undercover anymore. I think my brain hasn't realized this is all *my* reality. It's nice to have you with me. I'm sure it'll catch up to me sooner or later." Charlie finished looking under the red velvet armchair in the corner and moved over to the bed.

Deep in the darkness underneath the tattered box spring, Charlie spotted a rectangular shadow. She laid flat on her stomach and reached her right arm under the bed. The napkins around her wound fell off. Her fingers found a hard corner, and she knew it was the briefcase. With some finagling, she managed to scoot the briefcase closer until her fingers were able to grip the edge and pull it out into the light. She reached back under the bed and retrieved her interim bandage.

"Got it," Charlie said. She picked up the briefcase and held it out towards Debra.

Debra glanced over.

"That looks like hell," Debra said, her eyebrows raised.

"I'm told it holds my family secrets," Charlie said with an ominous tone and a small shrug. She was starting to enjoy Debra's enthusiasm and felt herself trying to match her energy. She was also disgusted by her injury and needed a shower.

Either that or I'm about to go insane trying to process everything!

"Uh, Charlie. I'm excited and all, but I meant your cut. You're straight-out bleeding all over now. Let's go get you re-bandaged and you can tell me more about your hideous family secrets," Debra gestured to the door.

Charlie lowered her arms and nodded. The skin around her wound was burning and she wasn't fond of the feeling of blood dripping down her arm. She snagged a hand towel off the bathroom rack and held it under her forearm.

Debra and Charlie walked silently out of Greg's room

and down the hall to Charlie's room. Charlie let Debra in and then remembered the state she left her room. She blushed.

Unlike Greg's room, Charlie had clothes draped over every surface and a bathroom counter full of makeup and hair products. Her bed was unmade and a little divot in the middle showed exactly where Charlie had last slept. The room was chilly, and the drapes still drawn.

"Well, you can tell I wasn't expecting company," Charlie said, a deep red. She walked across the room and opened the curtains with one hand, letting in cloudy sunlight. "My house in Kellyville is tidy, but I don't have cupboards or drawers here to organize anything."

"Oh no, don't apologize. And while we're at it, remind me not to invite you to my house," Debra said clearing a space on the bed. "My son takes out everything I put away so one day I just stopped cleaning. I'm sure he'll grow out of it just in time for my daughter to grow into that phase."

Charlie smiled at Debra's expression as she talked about her children. She looked tired, but happy, complete, proud. Charlie wondered what that would feel like.

Charlie thought of Tim's dream, *"I had a dream about*

our daughter last night."

Unfortunately, they'd never had the chance to begin a family. Tim had died a week after his dream confession.

"I hope to experience that pride someday. I love hearing you talk about your children," Charlie said to Debra with a hint of sadness. Debra patted her shoulder and nodded her head, a comforting gesture. Both women smiled.

Charlie broke out of her thoughts and handed the briefcase to Debra. She tried to call Jessica but after nine rings, hung up.

"Here, I'm dying to know what was worth stealing this case for, but my hair is a disaster and I'm afraid I've bled on everything I'm wearing. Dictate what you find while I take a quick shower." Charlie turned to walk towards the bathroom then froze.

I've ruined my clothing. They're completely trash. And yet...somehow...not once have I considered how Mother would have reacted. Or how I might repair the clothes.

"You okay?" Debra asked, standing up from the bed where she'd sat and trifled through the briefcase. She put her hand on Charlie's shoulder.

Charlie realized tears were sliding down her cheek. She

sniffled. Debra squeezed her shoulder lightly then patted her arm.

"Just been a weird day, Deb," Charlie replied with a slight smile. "But honestly, despite my partner lying to me about who he is, possibly even having murdered my fiancé, being kidnapped—again—saved by James, also again, and finding out Mother tried to warn me about Greg...the same mother who abused and broke me...despite all this, I'm sort of okay. Thanks for being here."

Charlie stepped in the shower and allowed the tears to stream down her cheeks.

#

Charlie stood in the shower rinsing away pieces of hay, shards of bricks, dried blood, and the drama of the day. She began planning while listening to Debra. First, Charlie planned to try Jessica again and if she didn't answer this time, she'd call Boyd and make sure he checked in on her. It wasn't like Jessica to not be available by phone for this long. Second, she and James should assume Greg would return to the warehouse and make a plan to trap him.

Debra, oblivious to Charlie's planning, sat on the bed loudly announcing items as she pulled them out of the briefcase. Some were repeats of the things Charlie saw before Greg broke into her hotel room and subdued her.

"There's a drawing of your family tree. Bunch of only-child families. Greg is your cousin according to this drawing. How crazy is that? I knew he didn't look like a Paul. Oh, this is such a cute metal semi truck toy! Says "Tucker Trucking" across the trailer. Hmm, here's a sealed letter that says, "Charlie" across it—beautiful cursive! I'll leave that one for you. Oh, this is a fascinating newspaper article!" Debra held up a newspaper article, forgetting Charlie wasn't looking. She laughed at herself then sobered again as she read further. "It talks about the incident at Tucker Trucking in 1968—they call it an accident. Two men died in a fight inside the warehouse: Hank Winslow—that's your dad?—and Lester Winslow— Greg's dad? Look like that's when James' dad, Peter, took over the company. Wow, it appears the funeral for your dad was well-attended, but this article says, 'The wife and child of the late Hank Winslow were not in attendance.' Wonder why your mom didn't want to go?"

Debra looked up as Charlie came out of the bathroom, her curly hair dripping water.

Charlie felt like she'd done as much planning as she could without James' input and not knowing the layout of the warehouse. She was wearing clean clothes and she'd properly bandaged her arm.

"One towel is not enough for any bathroom, but it feels good to be clean," Charlie said sitting down on the bed next to Debra and the briefcase. She used the damp towel to scrunch water out of her hair, defining her curls.

"My mom was not a good person in my childhood," Charlie said with a shrug. She pointed at the article in Debra's hand about the warehouse accident.

"It's weird talking about something that affected me so greatly but up until yesterday, I had no memory of it at all. Mother moved us one day and never talked about my dad or the company. I had little flashbacks here and there, but Mother hated talking about it. Honestly, she'd get violent when I would ask. The nightmares of this place were repetitive and brutal," Charlie said.

Why was Mother so angry with the world? What made her change her mind and try to reconnect with me? Then in her dying words, warn me about an insane cousin? Did she leave the tip about Greg lying his way into the FBI?

"We need to get back to the warehouse," Charlie said. She walked over to the safe planning to retrieve her gun.

"You know, you probably own part of that company," Debra said with a sly grin. She jumped up from the bed. "I can see it now...you and James, loading trucks and bossing around employees. And K - I - S - S..."

"Oh Debra!" Charlie turned to watch Debra do a silly dance and they both laughed. "So many blank spots in my memory are filling in seeing these photographs. The crazy thing is I didn't even realize there *were* blank spots. My relationship with Mother overshadowed anything good that happened in my early childhood. I just assumed it'd always been hell," Charlie said.

Debra gave Charlie a quick hug then reached back in the briefcase. She pulled out a weathered, white envelope that had the words "OPEN FIRST" scrawled in messy cursive with black ink.

"I saw the big envelope with beautiful script that says, "Charlie", but I didn't notice this one. The handwriting is similar, but much sloppier. Have you read this yet?" Debra held up the envelope.

"No, every time I pick it up, something happens," Charlie said eyeing the envelope. "And I don't think I was ready, either, but I'm prepared. Let me get my gun, first."

Charlie reached for the safe as she was showered with splinters. A large force shoved the motel door open and surged inside. Two small pieces of the door remained on the hinges; the rest of the door flew in shards across the room. A large human stomped over the hallway threshold and across the worn carpet directly towards Charlie. Debra jumped up and ran to the corner. Charlie turned to face a man three times her size.

"Neil," Charlie stated, recognizing the son of the gangster, Hen, she and Greg put away a handful of weeks ago. She clenched her fists and planted her feet, wishing she'd tried four seconds earlier to get her gun.

Neil didn't speak, just crossed the remaining distance in one step and swung his fist in the air, aiming for Charlie's face but Charlie ducked and sidestepped. Debra squealed from the corner of the room, the telephone receiver in her shaking hand.

Neil turned to see where the noise came from. Charlie

took advantage of the distraction. She bowed into the side of Neil's stomach with her shoulder, trying to set him off balance. Neil chuckled as Charlie tried to push him unsuccessfully with all her strength. He grabbed her hair and yanked her backwards, tipping her head to look him in the face. Charlie gritted her teeth against the pain and stared Neil in the eyes. His brown eyes were yellowed and bulging, clearly a side effect of long-time drug use.

"I don't like being told what to do, lady. But that's what I have to do for being set free. You and your agency are suckers, you know? Don't even understand how many of you we have on our side," Neil bragged.

Charlie collapsed into the floor, attempting to use her own weight to get out of his grip. Instead, she felt some of her hair rip and Neil tightened his grip. She dangled from her hair for a moment then put her feet back under her body, trying to relieve the pressure on her head.

Neil laughed at her pain. Raising his right arm into the air, he tightened his fist.

"No!" Debra yelled and a shatter of glass poured onto Charlie's head. Neil released his grip on Charlie's hair, and she dropped to the floor. Neil turned around to face

Debra. A wicked smile spread across his face; his eyes danced. Debra dropped the remaining parts of the table lamp she cracked over Neil's head and backed into the wall behind her, her lips parted in fear.

"Oh fun, a two-for-one. He'll have to pay me more," Neil said with excitement as he took a menacing step towards Debra. He raised his hands and curled his fingers, a bear confident in his size and ready to strike.

The sound of a cocking gun caused all three to pause and look toward the open doorway of the small motel room.

Jessica stood there with her right pointer finger on the trigger and a confident expression of perfect aim. She stood in the hallway, her body stiff and her face worried. Three more local police officers gazed calmly at Neil with their guns raised.

"Jessica!" Charlie said with relief, happy to see Jessica was alright. Debra went from fear to a smile as she realized this woman and all the guns were on Charlie's side.

Knowing he'd be dead in an instant if he moved, Neil raised his hands and let out a growl of frustration in defeat. He glanced back at Charlie, still sitting on the floor rubbing her head.

"Next time, Bitch. Next time, you're all mine. I don't care what he says…you and me…we've got a date." Neil winked and pursed his lips at Charlie as an officer approached Neil cautiously. Charlie wrinkled her nose at the thought of his intentions. One police officer lowered his weapon, removed silver handcuffs from his duty belt, and rattled off accusations and Miranda rights as he tried to stuff Neil's meaty wrists in the handcuffs. He finally gave up and asked another officer for his cuffs because Neil couldn't get his arms close enough behind his back to chain both wrists.

The other officer kept his gun locked on Neil as Jessica holstered her Glock and stepped around the large assailant and the two officers still trying to wrangle his wrists.

Jessica knelt by Charlie and touched her shoulder. Her straight dark-brown hair hung freely down her back. She wore a black and white striped pencil skirt and black blazer with a light cream sleeveless shirt underneath.

"Are you alright? I'm so sorry I wasn't here earlier," Jessica said eyeing Charlie's hair strands strewn across the floor.

"Yeah, we're okay. That hurt like a mother, but I've had worse ideas," Charlie said with a pained smirk, thinking of willingly drinking a tainted bar drink. "Debra, are you alright? That was very brave."

Debra tiptoed past Neil and the police guns and kneeled by Jessica and Charlie.

"Thank you, I'm sorry it didn't work as expected. It always works in the movies!" Debra said exasperated. She was shaking and pale, but calm. "Your hair..."

"Real life is never like a movie, Debra, but I appreciate you getting his sweaty fingers out of my hair," Charlie said kindly, rubbing her scalp again. She pointed from Jessica to Debra with her other hand. "Jessica, meet Debra, she is the mother of the child Greg rescued from the road. Debra, Jessica is my point of contact at the Albany field office. Debra knows my real name."

"Hi, Jessica," Debra said with a small wave then looked back at Charlie with a nervous expression. "Charlie, you clearly knew this man, but what did he mean when he kept referring to another he? '*He* owes me more' and 'I don't care what *he* says'. Who is '*he*'?"

"Nice to you meet you. Well, it's public record now, so I can tell you," Jessica explained. "Neil was out on bail awaiting his trial. Apparently, he'd agreed to turn on his father, Hen, in exchange for the chance at bail. What the news didn't report was Neil didn't check in with his parole officer this morning and I had a feeling. I tried to call you a couple of hours ago but with no answer, I jumped in the car. As I pulled into the motel parking lot, the local PD said they got a call from a woman inside about a break in, and I knew it was likely Neil. Thank you for the call, Debra."

Debra blushed. Charlie looked over at Debra with respect.

"You got a call in during all that? I'm impressed, Debra," Charlie said.

"I didn't get to finish the call, I just yelled out our location and problem and then grabbed a lamp," Debra said. "I'm guessing this guy has something to do with one of your cases."

"Yeah, he's from a case a few months ago. And to answer your question, I have no idea what *he* Neil is referring to. We haven't had a double agent in our office as long as I've been in the FBI."

Charlie looked over at Jessica with her eyebrows raised. "Care to hazard a guess on who *he* is?"

"It could be Greg, Charlie," Jessica said apologetically. "I know we don't want to make any assumptions, but it sort of makes sense. I can't talk about a few of them now, but Greg has been around for a lot of bad or strange things that have happened."

Neil let out a demonic cackle and the three women looked over at him. Charlie felt goosebumps form on her arms and Debra twitched. Two officers were leading him from the room when Neil looked back at Charlie with a sneer.

"He'll be here for you himself next, I bet. Just wait," Neil continued to laugh as he was shoved out the doorway and down the carpeted hallway.

21

Finding the Key

"WELL, THAT GUY is creepy," Debra said as the women listened to Neil's laughter echo down the hallway.

"I'll have him transferred to a facility far away and make sure I'm contacted if anybody talks to him," Jessica said in disgust. "We're going to figure out who let him go and stomp that son of a bitch into the ground."

Charlie laughed and Debra looked horrified.

"Ma'am, are you doing alright? I'll have to relocate you if you plan on staying another night," a hotel manager said appearing through the open doorway. She inspected the broken door with her hand on her chin.

"That's not necessary, I'm checking out. But thank you,"

Charlie replied.

Jessica raised her eyebrows then nodded. She looked at the night manager and said, "Another agent will be here shortly to settle the bill and finish the statements with the local officers. Thank you for your assistance."

The manager nodded, bending down to gather a shard of the door. She picked it up and lifted it towards the light, as if she were looking for fingerprints. With a grunt, she turned and left the room, dodging various detectives with yellow numbered signs.

Charlie picked herself up off the ground and looked around at the detectives rehashing the break in. She closed the briefcase and set it next to her suitcase then began gathering things from around the room. The other women helped.

"I heard about the tornado on the radio on my way here, and they said it was in Old Mill. I'm relieved you're okay," Jessica said reaching out for Charlie. She hugged her gently.

"I'm fine. I've been worried about you, too!" Charlie replied, hugging Jessica tightly.

It's so good to see you, Jess.

Jessica lifted Charlie's arm and surveyed the bandage.

"You weren't supposed to get injured on this case, Charlie."

"Boy, do I have so much to tell you," Charlie began with a tired grin. She recounted all the things that had happened since they last spoke at the diner, including rediscovering her childhood best friend and most likely being betrayed by her cousin, also known as, partner.

"He kidnapped you? And Greg is your cousin?" Jessica interrupted trying to process the whole story at once. "That means he lied and somehow got away with it. I knew the tip was credible! That vile man. He will pay for this!"

"I can't prove 100% that it was Greg that kidnapped me, but he did have the key on him. And we also have no real proof that he is my cousin, other than one person's word. And then I guess the tip you received, about Greg frauding his way into the FBI. When was the last time Greg checked in with you?" Charlie asked.

I'd trust James' word over Greg's any day, but I still need proof. If for some reason Greg is innocent, I'm requesting a new partner.

"Only you could be faced with a situation like this and

still defend the obviously guilty, Charlie," Debra piped up. She'd been clearing out the bathroom and had a handful of hair products. Charlie opened her powder bag, and Debra dropped the items inside.

"The last time was right after I told you I was sort of investigating Greg," Jessica said. "He called and said you were both going north to see about some murder investigation to see if it was related to Tucker Trucking and that you will both be offline for about a day or so. He sounded breathless and there was a lot of background noise on the line. I tried to call you directly to ask you about the tip but got the front desk attendant and left a message."

"Yeah, I got that message and tried to call you but neither you nor your assistant answered. The masked man broke into my room a few minutes later."

"I got called into a meeting with Boyd," Jessica said, shaking her head irritably. "Someone filed a complaint against me internally and Boyd was furious about this thing I'd supposedly done. We cleared it up, but it took hours."

"Bet it was Greg delaying you to keep Charlie from

finding out about this so-called trip he had planned," Debra interjected.

Charlie and Jessica nodded gravely.

Debra excused herself to call her husband to check in on the children.

"Well, I feel like a sitting duck staying in this room. What's our next move, Special Agent Winslow?" Jessica looked at Charlie hopefully.

"We don't get much training on rogue partners, Special Agent Chance," Charlie said with a snort. "But let's assume Greg is guilty for planning purposes. We should start at the warehouse. If Greg is here to avenge his father, we should get James involved. I nearly died from the hay and then a tornado—bet Greg didn't see that one coming. And now Neil...the foiled plans probably pissed him off. You should have seen him in the barn fighting James, Jess. Like a bull chasing a red muleta."

Charlie wished she'd known everything she knew now earlier in the day. She'd have helped James fight off Greg rather than sit there yelling at both of them like an idiot.

Debra hung up the phone.

"Charlie, my husband needs to go help with storm

cleanup first thing in the morning so I'm going to head home to be with the kids. I hate to leave, though. Is there anything else I can do for you?" Debra asked, clearly disappointed she'd miss out on anything else that might happen.

"You know, that's best, Debra," Charlie said. "Greg has no idea that you know anything, so you should be safe. And it's the middle of the night, I doubt anything will happen."

The worst stuff always happens overnight, Charlie thought. But she wanted to protect Debra.

"If you see Greg, just act like he's still Paul and I'm still June...no Jane...okay?" Charlie summarized.

Jessica smirked at Charlie's mistake.

Charlie walked across the room and put her arms around Debra.

"Thank you for everything. I'll be at Tucker Trucking if you need to call."

"Oh, I know you will, enjoy the visit," Debra said with a wink and started humming the sitting-in-the-tree song. Charlie rolled her eyes and laughed.

"Thank you for taking care of Charlie, Debra," Jessica

said, dipping her head.

Debra smiled, wished them good luck, and reminded Charlie to be careful. Then with a small wave, she grabbed her purse and walked out of the room.

"Let's get going, too," Charlie said closing her suitcase. She walked over to the safe. The buttons beeped as she entered the code and the door swung open.

Charlie paled. "The safe is empty, Jess. Greg must have my gun."

"I have mine, Charlie. Let me change into jeans then we can leave. If Greg is coming undone, he won't go down without a fight, and I'd rather not do that in a pencil skirt," Jessica said, walking to her FBI-issued CrownVic to retrieve her duffle.

The drive back to the warehouse was somber. Jessica drove just over the speed limit and Charlie directed her turns. The roads were empty, most people safely asleep in their beds.

"So, this warehouse, your grandparents started it?" Jessica asked.

"I guess so," Charlie replied, lifting the briefcase. "There are photographs of them in this briefcase. That's where my middle name came from, too. When I first met James at the diner, he kept calling me June, remember? How funny it must have been to him not realizing I had no clue who he was."

Charlie's stomach flip-flopped as she realized she was about to see James and likely spend the night with him.

"So how do we prove Greg's guilt or innocence?" Jessica asked. Charlie was grateful for the distraction from the direction her mind went.

"Well, like most masterminds, he'd probably love to brag if he concocted this whole thing. Once we find him, we just need him to talk."

"If we can get him in custody, even briefly, a simple DNA test can prove your relationship."

They both agreed that Greg was possibly already in the warehouse or would be soon.

Jessica pulled the car into the gravel parking lot and stopped by the side of the warehouse. James stepped out of a metal door and waved, a small smile playing on his lips.

His curls were freshly washed, and his clothes no longer torn and soaked through. He'd put on a red flannel shirt and dark jeans.

"That's the owner? Well, he's certainly attractive. Bet you don't think this case is purgatory anymore," Jessica snickered.

Charlie caught her breath as a wave of emotion swept over her.

This place feels like home. I feel like I belong here.

Charlie smiled back at James as he opened the passenger door of the car. Reaching out for her hand, he pulled her out of the seat and into his arms. He smelled fresh; a tinge of mint and lavender clung to his shirt. His sleeves were rolled up to the elbow, showing off his tanned arms. Charlie allowed herself to lean into his broad, strong chest. James tightened his arms around her and kissed the top of her head.

"I'm glad you're back, Charlie," James whispered.

Charlie tipped her head back and smiled up at James. Pushing up slightly on her toes, Charlie reached up and brushed her lips against his. She felt him smile beneath her lips then he pressed in and kissed her back.

Charlie heard Jessica clear her throat and stepped back with a sly smile. James moved his arm from around

Charlie's waist to draped lightly over her shoulders.

"Jessica, this is James. We were childhood buddies. He is also the owner of Tucker Trucking. Jessica is my contact, or 'handler' at the Albany office."

James reached out and shook Jessica's hand then his arm tightened around Charlie again.

"We, uh, had a bit of an incident at the motel. But Jessica arrived at the perfect time. Debra went home to be with her family," Charlie said in one breath. "We think Greg is losing his mind and is likely to be here now or soon. On one side, we have no *proof* that he's guilty of anything; on the other hand, there is substantial *evidence* that he at the very least was the one that took me from my room."

"I shut down production for tonight and sent a bunch of guys home just in case. Baron volunteered to stay behind and patrol the warehouse. No sign of Greg currently," James reported.

Greg has no idea what he'll be walking into if he tries. This is my home, my family, my friends; I will protect it all.

"We should probably wake up Boyd now, Charlie. Get some trained people out looking for Greg," Jessica said. "The local PD will write up a report about Neil and I have a stack of documents to fill out myself, but none of those will cross his desk for days. He'd want to know if his agent went rogue."

"I also know there is a family history of mental illness, Jessica. Greg is about the age his dad was when he lost it," James said.

"True," Charlie said. "I don't want to lose my job by reporting something with no concrete proof, but this is a personal matter, too. The history of this warehouse is clear, and it directly ties me to Greg," Charlie sighed. "Alright, Jess, call Boyd."

"This will be a fun call, he's still mad at me for doing the thing I didn't do," Jessica said rolling her eyes.

James led them into the warehouse and around several wood cutters and crates on the main floor. The only noise coming from the warehouse was the large fans hanging from the high ceiling circulating the air. One light flickered in the corner, but the lights throughout the warehouse were bright and steady. The floor was surprisingly clean, and the many shelves and aisles stacked were clearly labeled.

"It's weird how quiet it is in here right now," James said

over his shoulder. "Normally we have to wear ear protection." He nodded as a short man passed the group with a wave, a centurion protecting his post.

"That's Baron, my foreman. I think you met him the day of the explosion, Charlie. I explained to him who you are, and he told me he called it," James laughed. "He was proud of himself."

"Yeah, he told me I looked just like the family that started this business. At first, I thought he meant I was related to you in some way," Charlie said with a brief laugh. She was hyper aware of her hand in James' and was grateful that her initial assumption was wrong.

Charlie could feel Jessica's eyes on her and knew Jessica was dying to gush about Charlie's interest in James.

Another time, Jessica. I can't wait to tell you how I feel about him.

After weaving through a few more aisles James opened a metal door and allowed Jessica and Charlie to pass through before entering himself.

A blue carpeted hallway with three doors off both sides lay before them. Large, framed oil paintings of men sitting at desks lined the walls. Although there were no windows, the hallway had ample lighting. James walked around Charlie and stopped at the first door on the right and pulled out a key ring. After unlocking the door, he gestured to a phone and Jessica disappeared into the room. James turned and looked at Charlie who had frozen right inside the metal door. She was staring down the hallway.

The blue carpet. The hallway. It's warm in here. My nightmare...

"Charlie?" James asked worriedly.

"This hallway, I remember this hallway," Charlie began with a broken voice. Her mind was screeching through the past and this time, she didn't resist. "My dad's office was the second door on the left, I think. I used to run up and down this hall and drive Mother crazy. But Dad would tell her to let me be. And Uncle—oh my goodness—Uncle Peter!—your dad!—would throw me over his shoulder and take me on the warehouse floor to see the other workers when Mother and Dad would fight. Where have these memories been all this time?" Charlie looked at James with a bewildered expression. She'd finally found the key to a long-locked filing cabinet deep in her heart. Keeping her eyes on James as if he supplied her confidence, she turned the key to her childhood lock and memories came flooding back.

James and her playing tag on the rocky driveway. The construction of the house behind the warehouse—it was supposed to become Hank and Patricia's house. James and Charlie exploring the offices and finding Lester's hidden beer stash and him threatening to tell her dad they were trespassing and them all agreeing to just keep quiet. Lester showing off his newborn son, Greg. Lots of closed office conversations happened after that. Charlie was told not to wander anymore. Soon Mother and Charlie no longer visited the warehouse. Construction on the house stopped. Her mom getting a phone call and them rushing to the hospital. Being told she wouldn't see her dad anymore. The tailor shop and the abuse. Her mom waking her up in the middle of the night and a long car ride with few of their belongings. Then Envert Trailer Park in Cincinnati. Fighting her way through her childhood. Constantly feeling like she was missing something, but until now, not remembering what. Charlie thought she'd found what she was looking for once she joined the FBI—

an opportunity to keep people from doing bad things. That would make her feel whole. But now she knew she was just hiding out. Avoiding the past. Thinking just moving forward and putting herself in constant dangerous situations would make up for everything that she was lacking.

Family, that's what I've been missing. My entire past, my connections, my roots. The reasons I'm me.

Charlie reached out, afraid she might fall under the weight of the memories. James grabbed Charlie's hand and pulled her against his chest. He wrapped his arms around her.

22

Always Be Ready

"BOYD SAID HE will send a few agents to search for Greg," Jessica said, returning to the hallway. She noticed Charlie buried in James' arms and raised her eyebrows. "As Charlie pointed out, we don't have concrete evidence on anything related to Greg—other than a tussle with James—so Boyd is hesitant to involve the local police at this point," Jessica explained when she returned to the hallway. "How dare we possibly disgrace the FBI to save an FBI agent."

Charlie straightened from James' arms and smiled up at him.

"I'm okay," Charlie said. "I don't know how I managed to repress so much. I think I was afraid of what I might find, and I wasn't wrong. It's painful. How our family broke, and mom never recovered. Well, until she did, and I refused to allow her back. But I must live with that choice."

I'll plant a tree near my garden as an apology to mom for not giving her a chance.

Charlie glanced over at Jessica.

"I kind of already let James know why I'm here," Charlie said. "He admitted that at one point, my grandpa was engaged in illegal activities, but my dad and James' dad ended the nefarious shipments, which cost my dad his life," Charlie paused as a wave of sadness hit her.

How sad to kill somebody out of monetary greed. Lester took so much from me and my family. But I would never consider revenge. And I certainly wouldn't take it out on his kid. How does Greg see this ending?

"James, an unknown source has accused you of running an illegal shipping rift out of your warehouse," Charlie continued. She wanted to know for sure. "Although we have reason to believe these to be false allegations, if the FBI were to open a full investigation into this claim, would you be able to provide proof that you are not engaged in any illegal activities?" Charlie asked feeling a little silly. Her whole being knew he was innocent, but she had to gauge his reaction.

James chuckled, seemingly relieved at the question.

Completely innocent. Charlie wanted to crumple into James' arms again.

Jessica folded her arms and leaned back onto the door frame, watching another episode of the James and Charlie soap opera.

"If you'd asked me two weeks ago, I'd have said an emphatic yes. Now it's a little more complicated since someone blew up my records building. While I have current records on local hard drives, the older records were all paper. I've retrieved anything that was salvageable from that building and put it in boxes, but haven't had time to go through the pieces," James with a shrug.

"We can have our forensic team take a look at the fragments," Charlie suggested with a glance at Jessica.

Jessica nodded at Charlie, "Yeah, we can make that work."

Suddenly the hallway lights turned off.

The windowless hallway became so dark the air felt twenty degrees warmer. Everybody froze, trying to adjust their eyesight.

A stifling blackness wrapped around their bodies as if buried in sand.

Charlie mumbled something then sucked in a sharp breath.

"Charlie?!" James reached out for Charlie in the black air, but his hands touched nothing. Where she'd been moments before, only heavy darkness.

A door slammed; the wooden sound pulsed through their ears.

"James? Where's Charlie?!" Jessica fumbled in the darkness and found James' arm.

"Charlie!"

The silent response sounded like eight-foot ocean waves crashing onto a rocky shore.

"In the office, I have a flashlight, follow me!" James guided Jessica through the darkness back into the office. He stopped her by a desk and felt his way around the wooden surface. He slid open the top door. After shuffling a few items noisily around in the drawer, his hands landed on a cool metal cylinder.

James turned the flashlight on and pointed the light

towards Jessica. She had her gun pressed between her palms, the safety off. Her expression grim but calm. Jessica turned and walked towards the hallway.

"Let's find that son of a bitch."

#

I didn't even hear him coming, Charlie chastised herself.

Greg had appeared out of nowhere and pressed his pocketknife under Charlie's right rib cage, making her wince.

"Follow me or I shoot James," Greg whispered barely audible in her right ear. She'd felt the cool steel of a gun on her left shoulder by her ear. She nodded and he grabbed her right elbow, knife still in hand. Dragging her along, they'd ran down the hallway to another door. She heard James call out for her and wanted to yell, but Greg pushed the knife further and sliced her skin. Her eyes watered against the pain, but she forced herself to stay quiet.

They'll find me.

A series of pitch-black hallways later, Charlie had lost

track of where they were. For all she knew, they were walking in one big circle. She remembered the main hallway, but none of the other areas were familiar. Greg stepped deftly. He knew the layout and obviously had a plan.

Charlie managed not to trip despite the fast pace Greg was leading her. A final door and the two emerged back into the warehouse in-between two rows of floor to ceiling metal shelves full of wooden crates. Red emergency lights cast an eerie glow throughout the silent floor. The fans were no longer spinning. There was no movement.

Where is the foreman? Did James and Jessica follow her? James would be able to move deftly through the dark.

Charlie glanced back at Greg as he pocketed the knife, still attached to the CrownVic keyring, and took off what looked like binoculars strapped over his head then tossed them to the side of the aisle.

Night vision goggles. How long has Greg been planning this moment? Guess the story of Lester is true, Greg has officially lost it.

Greg's always-perfect hair stood on end, his face showed off an unshaved chin. He was wearing an aged black hoody and black athletic pants. Charlie had never seen him so disheveled. She felt the hairs on her neck reach for the ceiling.

Greg grabbed Charlie's elbow again and pushed her forward. They walked through three long aisles then turned left in what appeared to be the main walkway. Charlie saw a short man lying face down in the middle of the main aisle, unmoving.

"Greg! What did you do!" Charlie cried out, grieving the innocent man and hating the idea of James finding his foreman dead.

"Shh! Keep walking!" Greg whispered loudly and pushed the gun into the soft spot of her lower back. Charlie jerked away but started walking again. A long-time employee, Baron did not deserve this kind of ending. Charlie shuddered in rage.

Save your energy, Charlie. Save the anger. Wait.

Seven more aisles down the main walkway and Greg stopped Charlie. He pointed to a shadowed corner just beyond the edge of the last of the aisles. She looked up at the end of the aisle and saw a 27 painted in white on the metal. There were no emergency lights or windows in this corner of the warehouse.

"Go on. Sit with your back against the wall," Greg demanded.

Charlie nodded and stepped forward. Keeping her head straight, she moved her eyes left and right, up and down, looking for any kind of weapon she could grab.

"Don't try anything, Charlie; I have the gun," Greg warned as he followed Charlie into the deep grey shadow, his footsteps echoing in the silent room.

That's what I get working with a partner for two years, he knows my habits and tactics. I'll find a way to surprise you, Greg. You won't win this one. I at least have my full mind to work with.

"I don't understand, Greg. We're partners! I thought you died in that tornado! Are you okay?" Charlie asked, pretending to be concerned. She stopped at the wall and turned around, leaning against the cool concrete, but delayed sitting and tried to get him to start talking. "We searched for you after the tornado."

Greg responded by letting out one short burst of noise; something between laughter and a bark.

"Sure, Charlie, whatever. Even if this *had* been a real

case, you screwed it up the moment you laid eyes on James. Some partner!" Greg spit back. "Can't believe your mom used to work at that diner, dammit. Should have never saved that damn kid!"

Charlie couldn't see his facial expression in the shadows, but she imagined his face was red, like back at the motel.

So, Greg didn't know about mom's relationship with the diner. No wonder he was so angry that day. Where is James? I must keep Greg talking.

"A real case? What is that supposed to mean?" Charlie asked, still looking around for a weapon. She felt calm considering she was the only one without a weapon. She knew Greg was maniacal, but did he really want to kill her? He'd kidnapped her and tied her up, sure, but probably didn't know about her hay allergy.

"For being so smart, you're pretty dumb. So many things happen right in front of you, and you are oblivious. I'm the one that called in this so-called tip about James. I needed you here," Greg went silent. He seemed to be waiting for something.

Charlie thought about her dad, the warehouse, her mom, James... *Greg isn't wrong about me blocking out my past. But not anymore. What does he want with me?*

"Why'd you keep me away from here if you wanted me here?" Charlie asked with her hands up in the air.

Make sense about something, Greg!

"It had to be the right time, Charlie. And I wanted you a bit more incapacitated. But everybody keeps screwing up my plans," Greg said. His hair seemed to frizz more by the second, and there was a dribble of drool on his chin from speaking through his teeth.

Where has his mind gone? Where's the put-together, smooth-talking frat boy?

"You sent Neil?"

"I've been working with Hen for years. He let me live during the Inona case in exchange for keeping him out of jail. I was running out of ways to keep him out of jail, so I told him we had to up our agreement. He promised to kidnap you and bring you here, and you walked right into it. But he was wrapped up in so much more with that damn girl, he failed, and I had to take him down. Then his idiot son decided to play, too. I made a deal with him, but he failed, too. Soon the whole family will be dead, and I will no longer be in their debt," Greg said. His eyes caught a slight glint of the red emergency lights and glowed an ember coal.

Charlie felt like a demon could leak out of him any moment.

"You are so easy to read, Charlie. You're so focused on not remembering your past that you forget to see your present," Greg continued.

"Okay, point made, but what are we doing here? You just going to shoot me like your father did to mine?" Charlie asked.

"Ah, so you do remember something. Look around, Charlie. This is where our dads had their final fight. Everything I've done has led up to this moment. I blackmailed your previous partner to leave, took over his role to get close to you. That was easy, he was into some iffy things. But you still wouldn't give me the time of day, so I created a reason for you to need me," Greg said proudly.

No. Charlie already knew the answer but had to ask anyways. She had to make him say it.

"What reason? Oh no, no, no...You killed Tim?" Charlie asked, trying desperately to maintain her patience. She knew she was close to letting her emotions take over.

Wait, the voice reminded her.

Never had Charlie felt so vulnerable. This man had been close to her, seen her cry, hugged her when she grieved. Charlie shivered. Not knowing who'd murdered Tim had eaten at her for two years. She was a good FBI agent, but even she couldn't solve that crime. She always felt that Tim's corpse was yelling at her to know.

And Greg had been the one to pull the trigger.

"I did, Charlie. It was too easy," Greg bragged. "He begged for me to not hurt you, that he'd do whatever I wanted. 'Sure,' I'd said, just to get him to kneel in the entry way. I wanted to make sure you saw him immediately. It was your dating anniversary, after all, wasn't it?" Greg sneered.

Charlie forgot Greg had a gun and lunged at him with years of rage coursing through her. She let her emotions take over.

Charlie's shoulder contacted Greg around the waist, and they both fell into the crates behind him. Greg grunted and reached for his pocket where he'd stored the knife. Charlie stepped back, braced her feet, and swung her fist.

Greg leaned back, but Charlie's fist connected with the edge of his chin. Greg grunted as his head jolted to the right. He opened the knife in one swift motion with his left hand. He stepped into Charlie as she reset for another punch, catching her across the top of her left shoulder with the sharp blade.

Charlie cried out and stepped back, blood showing on her sleeve immediately. She sucked in a deep breath and stepped in again, this time connecting her fist with Greg's stomach. He folded over and she kicked his left hand, dislodging the pocketknife from his grasp. The knife skidded across the floor, scraping across concrete, and stopped moving under the metal shelving of aisle 27. Greg roared as he stood up and lifted his right hand. He hit Charlie on the side of her head with the butt of the gun and a cracking sound echoed in the shadows.

Charlie fell limp onto the grey floor.

23

Fight Hard

"CHARLIE!"

Charlie felt a dark cloud hovering in her vision.

I know that voice.

"Charlie!"

Wake up, Charlie. Charlie. Her dad. She heard his voice.

Charlie, it's time to get up.

Charlie blinked. She was lying on a cold, concrete floor. She couldn't move. Her eye struggled to adjust to the darkness that loomed above her.

Greg killed Tim.

Charlie remembered. Tears met her eyes, and she

squeezed them shut feeling a dirty pond form by her ear.

Greg killed Tim.

"Charlie!"

James? James! No, run, run, James!

Charlie couldn't move. Couldn't speak. She hoped her heart cried loud enough he would hear her.

Charlie forced her eyes open again. She saw booted feet pass her line of vision towards the end of the aisle, walking quietly towards the voice.

Run, James!

"Charlie!"

A gun shot echoed off the concrete walls and a thump told Charlie a body had fallen. Charlie's conscious became more alert, but she didn't move. She listened. She cried.

"James!" Charlie heard Jessica yell in a panic from a distance.

Did James get shot?

Charlie was lying on her stomach with her head facing the metal shelving. She focused on keeping her breathing calm; she didn't want to alert Greg that she was awake.

James. James. Charlie couldn't stop the silent tears.

Breathe, Charlie. Focus. Wait.

In...out.

What is that?

Charlie saw a shadow in the shadows. A small shape under the metal shelving.

Don't move yet, she heard the voice say as she tried to choke back the tears. *Gather yourself.*

"I see you, Jessica!" Greg called. He was somewhere a few feet away from Charlie's feet, near where she heard the thump after the gun shot. Charlie heard him move farther away so she reached out towards the shadow and her fingertips connected with cold metal.

Greg's knife!

Charlie used her fingertips to gather the knife in her palm then brought it up against her chest resuming her previous position. She cautiously glanced down towards the footsteps and saw James lying on his side, his back to Charlie. His arms were wrapped around his stomach and blood pooled around his rib cage. She couldn't tell if he was breathing and felt a panic rise in her throat. She needed to get to James right away and stop the bleeding, but Greg was standing over him, watching.

Breathe, Charlie. Breathe!

Charlie took a deep breath and looked away. She fought the urge to scream at the top of her lungs. She felt completely helpless.

"You shot James, Greg," Jessica called out from somewhere past the end of the aisle, her voice cracking. "You killed the foreman. Charlie is down. What's your goal here? Why don't you put down the gun and we can talk about what you need. Get you the help you need."

Greg looked towards Jessica's voice and raised his gun. Slightly crouched, he took three small steps towards her voice, his shoulders relaxed, and his arms raised, gun level, hands steady. Charlie could see a sliver of Jessica at the end of the aisle through the metal slats and wooden crates.

Jessica, run! Get help!

Even as she thought it, Charlie knew Jessica would never leave her.

Sweet Jessica. A friend before she knew she could allow someone close. Jessica creeped into her heart without Charlie even knowing. Charlie realized how dear Jessica had become to her.

Charlie wanted to sob, to scream, to move. She couldn't

just lay here and let Greg hurt another person.

Stay still, Charlie, the voice reminded her. *You're not ready, yet.*

"Jessica, I liked you. I thought maybe we'd be something someday," Greg said. "Although we did have some fun, it was never enough for me." He momentarily sounded like a man nervously talking to his crush rather than the crazed man she saw before she'd been knocked out.

"You got me in trouble with Boyd!" Jessica responded in disgust. "And it was one night, Greg. Get over yourself."

"You weren't supposed to be here, Jessica," Greg said, his voice cracking. "But you had to go and launch that silly investigation on me, so I guess you dug your own grave here."

"How did you know I was looking into that tip?" Jessica asked.

She's buying time. She must know when the other agents are supposed to arrive! James, hold on!

"Everybody talks, Jessica. You know that. Everybody knew about us."

Eew, Charlie thought. Although she wasn't entirely

surprised.

"Why did you make Charlie come here, Greg? It was you that filed the tip on Tucker Trucking, wasn't it?"

Charlie heard a discreet sound of a bullet being loaded into a gun, and wondered if Greg heard it, too. She peeked through her eyelids and saw he hadn't changed his position. He still had his aim locked on Jessica through the slats of the crates—a shot only a well-trained agent could make.

Get him, Jessica!

"None of your business," Greg spat. "And lucky for me, my stupid aunt died before you could meet her in New York."

Charlie bristled. The final pieces of her conscious fully awake, she felt a flush of heat from her feet to her cheeks.

Mom filed the tip on Greg?!

Greg took two more steps then squatted down and leveled his gaze across the top of his outstretched hands, his gun pointed at a slot in the metal shelving, Jessica's right leg the target.

Greg loaded a bullet, not Jessica!

Another gunshot echoed through the silent warehouse

floor. Jessica yelped and fell to the ground, holding her right thigh.

It's time, Charlie.

Charlie flashed back to finding Tim in the entry way of their house. His open, bleeding chest. She thought about her dad and mom fighting in the office at the warehouse. Chasing James through the parking lot in the spring rain. James saving her from the hay.

Now, Charlie!

Dizzy and unstable, Charlie pushed herself to standing.

The day she chose to leave her mom's abusive household. The moment she joined the FBI and cadet graduation day. Her first assignment.

I am strong. I am capable.

Grasping the knife in her clenched fist, she steadied and turned towards Greg.

Finding James again. Their first kiss. James asking her to stay. His arms around her.

I am capable of forgiveness.

With a low growl, Charlie took four large steps and jumped on Greg's back, burying the knife below his right shoulder.

"I won't let you hurt anybody else!" Charlie roared gripping him with all her strength.

Greg screamed and stood up.

"You can't take anymore from me!" Charlie yelled, wrapping her legs tight around Greg's waist to keep from falling off. She lifted the knife out, ready to plunge into his skin again. Greg turned around harshly, flinging Charlie off onto the hard ground near where Jessica lay. Charlie grunted as she landed onto the concrete, the knife once again skidding across the floor.

Greg raised his gun at Charlie again. His nostrils flared.

Charlie glared at him, her chest heaving.

"This is what you deserve, Charlie. This is what your dad deserved, too! He took everything from us. My dad didn't deserve to die. He had a plan, and your stupid parents ruined it! He was going to leave a legacy. Well, now I'm going to leave a legacy. I will build this empire back!" Greg lowered the gun towards Charlie's face.

Jessica grunted from the end of the aisle and shoved her gun across the floor towards Charlie. Charlie grabbed the gun and shot Greg in the right shoulder.

Greg yelled out in pain and surprise and fell to the

ground, dropping his gun. He gripped his shoulder with his left hand. Looking up at Charlie, he narrowed his eyes.

"This isn't over, Charlie. I'll get to you. I always know where you are. I know where you sleep. I know when you're in that stupid garden of yours. I'll make you suffer like I did to Tim."

Charlie had heard enough. She stood up and raised the gun at Greg.

"Oh, you're going to shoot me, Charlie? Ha, you don't have the guts," Greg taunted.

Charlie cocked the gun, her breathing settled.

"You're too nice. You believe in the system still, it's sick. If you only knew all the strings I've pulled and all the lies I've gotten away with. Maybe then you wouldn't believe anymore," Greg continued.

Suddenly James began to stir.

"No, Charlie, no," James mumbled.

"James?" Charlie glanced at James and back at Greg. Greg seemed surprised that James was moving.

Keeping the gun leveled at Greg, Charlie sidestepped over to James.

James coughed and moaned. He lifted his hands off his

stomach to show a gaping wound and seeping blood.

"Oh James," Charlie said sadly. She glanced at Greg again who seemed frozen in shock, staring at James. She set the gun down and pushed James' shirt over the wound and applied compression. She glanced over at Jessica. She was pale, but awake, watching Charlie.

"Jess, hold on!" Charlie encouraged then choked back another sob as her eyes landed on James. "James, stay with me. I...I need you."

"Charlie, Charlie," James said drifting out of consciousness.

He's lost too much blood.

Charlie glanced up as she heard a bullet load into the chamber of a gun. Greg stood up, gun in his left hand, a maniacal sneer raised his lips. He moved his finger to the trigger.

"Greg, no. Please," Charlie begged.

"This ends now, Charlie." Greg said.

Charlie looked Greg in his eye.

Greg smiled. His eyes a deep emerald blue.

I'm ready. I found my past. I found love. I found me.

A single tear rolled down Charlie's cheek.

A bullet discharged from a gun and Charlie dropped onto James' body, her arms stretched limp over his head.

24

Scars Heal

Two days later

"I GUESS I have to accept that this time, you saved me," James said with a gentle smile.

Charlie smiled back and put her hand on James' shoulder. He'd just been wheeled back to his room after a second surgery. She'd been pacing frantically in his hospital room expecting every negative outcome for four hours while waiting for him.

The first surgery to remove the bullet had been unsuccessful. James' heart rate had kept dropping and the surgeon decided he needed to stabilize the patient before a second attempt was made.

"The doctor said they were able to remove the bullet from your ribcage this time. You're going to be okay, James." Charlie tried to speak without emotion, but his name caught in her throat, and she choked back a sob.

She pictured his face just yesterday, so pale, so vulnerable. The doctor's plan was effective, and James stabilized by early evening. Charlie had been ordered to sleep by the kind nurse, and she tried, but she found herself staring at James all night from the cot they'd rolled in for her. She'd pleaded out loud countless times with him to come back to her.

First thing this morning James had been cleared for surgery.

James reached his hand up and Charlie grasped his fingers tightly; the anesthesia still ruling James' consciousness.

"You've always been so brave, Charlie. When we used to play as children, I just wanted to protect you from anything that could hurt you. I knew then you were special. But now, now... I want you here with me my whole life. Will you stay with me?" James looked up at Charlie with hopeful but sleepy eyes.

Charlie chuckled and touched his chin.

"Sweetheart, you're drugged. Yes, yes, I'm here forever. You're stuck with me," Charlie responded. She brushed a dark strand of hair off his forehead and again admired his curls. James smiled and turned his head towards her touch.

"What happened, Charlie? Tell me again?" James asked, his eyes heavy. His hand dropped from Charlie's grasp, and she tucked the blanket around his arm while deciding how to respond.

"Greg was ready to shoot me. Jessica was bleeding profusely from her leg at the end of aisle 27. You had a gun shot to the rib cage and were unconscious due to blood loss," Charlie began.

"Some knight in shining armor I am," James replied with a snort. Charlie smiled and put her hand on his blanketed arm.

You have no idea, my love.

"At the last minute, Jessica...Jessica shoved me her gun, but I couldn't do it, James. I couldn't shoot Greg. Then you came to momentarily, and I went to check on you. You're a little distracting, you know," Charlie traced his chin with her fingers. She could tell he was starting to drift back to sleep. She was pleased with the slight flush on his cheeks, a large change from the grey tint yesterday morning.

"Then Greg cocked his gun to let me know he had no hesitations," Charlie continued. "I was done for. I made peace with it. I found you again. I found *myself*. But you know what? It wasn't my time. Boyd had changed his mind after the call with Jessica and called in the cavalry. And right then...right when it was all over, he appeared." Charlie looked up at the ceiling and choked back another sob.

Jessica. I owe you so much. My friend, my confidant.

Jessica had managed to stay conscious long enough to pass Charlie the gun. Then she succumbed to bleeding out from a gunshot wound to her femoral artery. Jessica never got to see the result of her bravery.

Charlie allowed the heavy, wet tears to roll down her cheeks as she replayed the emergency responders announcing Jessica's time of death at the end of aisle 27. Charlie had screamed at the paramedics, told them to check again, that there's no way she's dead. They'd had to pull Charlie away, fighting, slamming her fists against their chest. Boyd had swept her into a hug while they both cried.

"I'm sorry about your friend, Charlie," James mumbled with his eyes closed. His hand once again sought out Charlie's touch.

She connected with his hand, his fingers caressing her palm, comforting her. She sucked in a shaky breath to slow the tears.

"My boss, Boyd, shot Greg in the right lower stomach, disabling him enough to contain him. He's got a lot of court dates and shaming news articles ahead of him. Well, so do I, I guess. Everybody is going to want to know more about us being cousins and our family history, and how Greg managed to infiltrate the FBI. It's a mess. As you can imagine, I'm on administrative leave for now. Boyd has been kind the last two days, I think he's hurting without Jessica, too. But I'm not sure he'll want me back in the Albany office," Charlie said, a startling realization to herself.

I haven't even considered how Greg's actions would affect me and my career. Do I even want to go back anymore?

"Maybe it's private security for me now," Charlie thought out loud. "That sounds nice. Play by my own rules, and pick my own damn cases."

James' breathing was rhythmic and comforting and Charlie realized he'd fallen asleep. She stared at his long, dark eyelashes and admired how his curly hair wrapped around the arch of his forehead just right. Charlie watched the rise and fall of his broad chest then leaned over his hospital bed and kissed his forehead, lingering. His lips raised in a smile and she gently kissed the corner of his mouth.

"Sleep sweet, my love," Charlie whispered. "I'll be here when you wake up."

"I want to see your garden," James mumbled. "I bet it's as pretty as you."

"I'd like that."

"I love you, Charlie."

"I love you, too."

Forever.

Epilogue

Two weeks later...

"I FIGURED IT out, Tim," Charlie said to the white gravestone. She'd thought she'd be crying, or angry, or dismissive. Instead, she felt calm. Okay-ish. She was happy to be back in Massachusetts and her porch overlooking the garden. She'd spend the last several days winterizing the garden with James sitting on the porch wrapped in a blanket watching her. He was healing fast and expected to be fully recovered within a month or so.

Charlie lifted her face to the cool winter air and closed her eyes.

"Greg killed you," Charlie said opening her eyes and exhaling, "which obviously, you already know. Turns out he was my cousin; who'd have thought?" Charlie paused. She leaned forward and traced the name of her late fiancé etched in the granite arch. "I'm sorry I didn't visit the past two years... I wanted to visit you once I had answers. You know how I am when I'm on a case... have to solve it! This one just took a weird, long turn I wasn't prepared for. I'm sorry that despite your sweet and gentle suggestions, I refused to investigate my childhood. You were right, you know. You'd have loved to hear that," Charlie smiled in memory, "but, mom left this imprint on me that I didn't understand. If I'd have been home for that phone call, and her telling me to look out for Greg, this whole thing could have been avoided. I won't apologize, because you told me that all the time, 'don't apologize, just take responsibility, Charlie'... that's what you'd say. I am now, Tim. Thank you."

The wind blew through the naked trees. Charlie shivered and knelt on the grave. She pulled her tweed jacket tighter around her body. Looking around she saw a handful of people braving the winter winds, checking on their deceased loved ones. A wet drop landed on Charlie's cheek, and she looked toward the dark sky. A heavy white snowfall began to mask the bleak landscape with a serene layer of silence. Charlie smiled again as she stood and straightened her coat.

"Goodbye, sweet Tim."

One Year Later...

"Charlie, it fits fine," James said, for the third time. "You've tried on everything in your closet. It's just Debra. She doesn't care what you wear. She thought you were a lowly writer; I highly doubt she's going to care if you're wearing silk or flannel."

Charlie glanced down the staircase at James. She was wearing one of James' white V-neck t-shirts and his sweatpants. James stared up at her with his hand spread apart. She couldn't help but smile down at his confused face.

"None of my clothes are proper anymore," Charlie complained with only slight sarcasm.

Seemingly deciding, James shook his head and climbed the stairs to meet Charlie on the upstairs landing. He stood behind her and spread his hands over her swollen belly.

"Look, you can obsess over thread patterns and material type once the baby is born. Your mom left you money that you've invested in our lovely house, why not hire a private tailor to get you some clothes you approve of? You've created an amazing team with your security business, and they're handling everything while you take care of yourself and our baby. Please find a way to be comfortable?" James whispered in her ear.

Charlie felt a shiver up her body that wasn't from cold and leaned her head back against his strong chest. Never in her life did she know a human could feel this content, despite the discomfort her changing body was experiencing. Her memories flashed to mom, drunk, throwing a can of beans at her eleven-year-old head because they were the wrong sodium level.

Never, Charlie thought. *Never will I do that to a child.*

Then Charlie pictured mom learning about Greg's lies and deciding to make the call to the FBI and in her final moments, warning her daughter to look out for a ruthless cousin.

She saved me, Charlie reminded herself. *I can't change my childhood, but I can appreciate who it made me and who I became.*

Turning towards James, Charlie buried her head in his chest as close as she could be with her belly between them.

"Thank you for saving me from myself, James."

James made a choking sound and Charlie looked up to his face. His eyes were shiny as a single tear rolled down his cheek. He reached up and held her chin, looking in her eyes.

"Charlie, I waited for you," James replied, "without realizing it. And maybe you did, too. But now, we're here. And together. And I love every moment." He released her chin and grabbed her tightly, pressing her body into his.

Charlie felt her own eyes fill up, her cheeks damp from her own tears.

A car horn sounded outside.

"Debra!" Charlie exclaimed drying her cheeks. She released her hold from James' waist and grabbed his head with both her hands. She kissed his lips then turned and descended the stairs with her left hand on the railing and right hand on her belly.

"Woah, slow down Charlie!" James laughed as he followed her down the stairs.

Opening the front door, Charlie stepped onto the front stoop and waved at Debra, Bill, and their two kids. Oliver was the first to exit the minivan.

"Aunt Charlie!" Oliver exclaimed running with his arms spread wide. Charlie caught him as he jumped from the final porch step and squeezed him tightly.

"Oliver, be gentle!" Debra called from the car as she unbuckled a wiggly one-year-old Rosie from her car seat.

"I've got her, Debra," Bill told Debra as he moved in front of her and gathered Rosie in his arms. "Go ahead."

Debra nodded and raced from the driveway, as fast as Oliver, and up the porch steps.

"Look at you!" Debra exclaimed. She looked at Charlie's face then glanced at her stomach and sucked in a breath. "You look beautiful, Charlie." Debra put her hands on Charlie's shoulders and gathered her in for a hug.

"Debra, I'm so glad you're here. This will be the best Thanksgiving ever!" Charlie replied as James stepped onto the porch. He took Oliver from Charlie and threw his arm over Debra's shoulder. Debra side-hugged James and watched Rosie chase a bunny into Charlie's garden.

"We have the best family, don't we?" Debra replied, holding Charlie's hand. Charlie felt tears form in her eyes again.

"Oh, stop it, I'm already weepy enough today!" Charlie said cry-laughing. She leaned into James, and he kissed her forehead. Oliver reached over and squeezed Charlie's neck.

Charlie smiled.

THANK YOU FOR READING MY NOVEL.

I APPRECIATE YOU.

OTHER THINGS I'VE DONE

Emotional Humidity. A Poetry Collection

Hardcover ISBN: 9798299331585

Paperback ISBN: 9798262435180

UPCOMING THRILLERS

A Man Too Soon

Heth School for Girls